HARRY MOON

WAND-PAPER-SCISSORS

by
Mark Andrew Poe

Illustrations by Christina Weidman

rabbit publishers

Wand-Paper-Scissors (Harry Moon)
by Mark Andrew Poe
© Copyright 2017 by Mark Andrew Poe. All rights reserved.

Rabbit Publishers
1624 W. Northwest Highway
Arlington Heights, IL 60004

Illustrations by Christina Weidman
Cover design by Megan Black
Interior design by Lewis Design & Marketing
Creative Consultants: David Kirkpatrick, Thom Black, and Paul Lewis

ISBN: 978-1-943785-59-9

10 9 8 7 6 5 4 3 2 1

1. Fiction - Action and Adventure 2. Children's Fiction
First Edition
Printed in U.S.A.

Harry, having a friend
like me has consequences.

~ Rabbit

Table of Contents

PREFACE

Halloween visited the little town of Sleepy Hollow and never left.

Many moons ago, a sly and evil mayor found the powers of darkness helpful in building Sleepy Hollow into "Spooky Town," one of the country's most celebrated attractions. Now, years later, a young eighth-grade wizard, Harry Moon, is chosen by the powers of light to do battle against the mayor and his evil consorts.

Welcome to the world of Harry Moon and his amazing adventures. Darkness may have found a home in Sleepy Hollow, but if young Harry Moon has anything to say about it, darkness won't be staying.

FAMILY, FRIENDS & FOES

Harry Moon

Harry is the thirteen-year-old hero of Sleepy Hollow. He is a gifted magician who is learning to use his abilities and understand what it means to possess the real magic.

An unlikely hero, Harry is shorter than his classmates and has a shock of inky, black hair. He loves his family and his town. Along with his friend Rabbit, Harry is determined to bring Sleepy Hollow back to its true and wholesome glory.

Rabbit

Now you see him. Now you don't. Rabbit is Harry Moon's friend. Some see him. Most can't.

Rabbit is a large, black-and-white, lop-eared, Harlequin rabbit. As Harry has discovered, having a friend like Rabbit has its consequences. Never stingy with advice and counsel, Rabbit always has Harry's back as Harry battles the evil that has overtaken Sleepy Hollow.

II

Honey Moon

She's a ten-year-old, sassy spitfire. And she's Harry's little sister. Honey likes to say she goes where she is needed, and sometimes this takes her into the path of danger.

Honey never gives in and never gives up when it comes to righting a wrong. Honey always looks out for her friends. Honey does not like that her town has been plunged into a state of eternal Halloween and is even afraid of the evil she feels lurking all around. But if Honey has anything to say about it, evil will not be sticking around.

III

Samson Dupree

Samson is the enigmatic owner of the Sleepy Hollow Magic Shoppe. He is Harry's mentor and friend. When needed, Samson teaches Harry new tricks and helps him understand his gift of magic.

Samson arranged for Rabbit to become Harry's sidekick and friend. Samson is a timeless, eccentric man who wears purple robes, red slippers, and a gold crown. Sometimes, Samson shows up in mysterious ways. He even appeared to Harry's mother shortly after Harry's birth.

Mary Moon

Strong, fair, and spiritual, Mary Moon is Harry and Honey's mother. She is also mother to two-year-old Harvest. Mary is married to John Moon.

Mary is learning to understand Harry and his destiny. So far, she is doing a good job letting Harry and Honey fight life's battles. She's grateful that Rabbit has come alongside to support and counsel her. But like all moms, Mary often finds it difficult to let her children walk their own paths. Mary is a nurse at Sleepy Hollow Hospital.

IV

John Moon

John is the dad. He's a bit of a nerd. He works as an IT professional, and sometimes he thinks he would love it if his children followed in his footsteps. But he respects that Harry, Honey, and possibly Harvest will need to go their own way. John owns a classic sports car he calls Emma.

Titus Kligore

Titus is the mayor's son. He is a bully of the first degree but also quite conflicted when it comes to Harry. The two have managed to forge a tentative friendship, although Titus will assert his bully strength on Harry from time to time.

Titus is big. He towers over Harry. But in a kind of David vs. Goliath way, Harry has learned which tools are best to counteract Titus's assaults while most of the Sleepy Hollow kids fear him. Titus would probably rather not be a bully, but with a dad like Maximus Kligore, he feels trapped in the role.

Maximus Kligore

The epitome of evil, nastiness, and greed, Maximus Kligore is the mayor of Sleepy Hollow. To bring in the cash, Maximus turned the town into the nightmarish, Halloween attraction it is today.

He commissions the evil-tinged celebrations in town. Maximus is planning to take Sleepy Hollow with him to Hell. But will he? He knows Harry Moon is a threat to his dastardly ways, but try as he might, he has yet to rid himself of Harry's meddling.

Kligore lives on Folly Farm and owns most of the town, including the town newspaper.

The Scariest Thing of All

There was plenty that was scary in Sleepy Hollow, including the gloomy town square and the Headless Horseman statue. There were weird, menacing creatures walking the sidewalks, just ready to creep you out. Most of the streets had eerie names. Witch Broom Road. Conical Hat Avenue. Even the weather was a bit out of the ordinary in Sleepy Hollow. It seemed that autumn was always in the air as the sweet, nutty, brown aromas of fall and Halloween wafted about. Yes, there was a lot of which to be scared. At Sleepy Hollow Middle School, however, the scariest thing of all was the students. This seemed especially true around Halloween, when competitive excitement ran high over who would win the Annual Scary Talent Show.

Harry Moon, an eighth-grade aspiring magician, would be a shoo-in for the win, as he was wonderful with table magic like card tricks, vanishing scarves, and pulling toy rabbits out of his top hat. But Titus Kligore, the school bully, had the resources and the sizzle to beat Harry Moon.

Last year, Titus and his buddies won the Scary Talent Show with a singing review of "Tonight We Party." They were only in seventh grade at the time, but they still won. Normally, the win was reserved for the eighth grad-ers. Titus's guys, the Maniacs, had dressed in classic monster gear—the Mummy, Frankenstein, the Werewolf, and Dracula. Their singing was pretty good too.

Titus's dad, Maximus Kligore, was not only the mayor of Sleepy Hollow, but he ran the most successful costume shop in town — Chillie Willies. Titus had had a big advantage over everyone else since Chillie Willies had dressed Titus and his friends in the most outrageous, horrifying outfits that money could buy. Besides, everyone was afraid of Titus. Who wanted to be stuffed in their locker by the Maniacs?

3

This year, pain-in-the-butt Titus planned to win again with a singing revue entitled "Let's Get Hysterical," comprised of movie monsters— Freddie, Jason, the Werewolf, and Jigsaw. But there was a chill in the air. Word had spread that Harry Moon was out to win the contest, which made Titus and the Maniacs crazy mad. Tenacious and hard-working, Harry had been practicing his magic tricks every night after school in the Performing Arts Center on campus.

Miss Pryor, the drama teacher who all the guys wished they could kiss (rumor had it that Titus had planted one on her lips last year on her birthday), was in charge of the Scary Talent Show. She had told her class that Harry Moon was the guy to watch.

"One day," Miss Pryor said, "Harry Moon could be as good as Elvis Gold."

"Weooo!" said many in the schoolroom. The class was astonished by the teacher's praise.

Elvis Gold was the most wonderfully magical magician in America. Just last week, Elvis Gold, locked in chains and frozen in a block of ice in the Hudson River, escaped certain death on screens all over the world. Harry had watched it dozens of times on his phone.

Titus Kligore did not enjoy hearing that Miss Pryor was glowing about Harry Moon. This meant competition for him. Titus was accustomed to getting his way and keeping control of the kids. He had to win the Scary Talent Show at any cost.

4

Titus Kligore had never liked Harry Moon one bit, which was not a good thing for Harry. Titus was huge—a good foot and a half taller than Harry. He had a ginormous head and broad shoulders. He was one of the first guys to be able to make a really loud whistle without using his fingers. He had learned that from his uncle, who, rumor had it, was in jail for stealing beers.

The worst of it was that Titus was reckless. His hormones were raging. He even had nine chin whiskers when he was in fourth grade. Now, in eighth grade, he was wildly out of control.

The only thing Titus did have under control was the way he moved. He didn't walk through corridors like the other guys—he swaggered.

It was this swagger that he was showing off later that day when he confronted Harry Moon outside of the cafeteria.

"Listen, runt," said Titus as he grabbed Harry by the collar outside the cafeteria. Titus slammed him against the wall. "I hear that Willow Wood is excited about you doing some smelly-butt tricks for them this Saturday night." Willow Wood was the old folks' home in Sleepy Hollow.

"That's funny," said Harry, wiggling out of Titus's grasp, "because I'll be on stage here Saturday night beating the pants off you!" Harry's stomach was churning, but he refused to reveal his fear to Titus Kligore.

As he headed to his class, Harry heard Titus's growl from over his shoulder. "You won't be on the Scary Talent Show stage if you know what's good for you."

Daylight saving time had ended, so it was dark when Harry Moon walked home from talent practice at the middle school. The wind was blowing, rattling the branches of the trees that lined the sidewalk. The wind was always stronger at this time of year. The gusts shook the last leaves from the trees until the branches were bare, reaching out to the gray sky like fingers on skeletons' hands. The yellow moon drifted behind the shaking branches like an unfolding nightmare.

It was almost Halloween in Sleepy Hollow, Massachusetts. For years, tourists had clogged the streets of the little burg, coming from all around the world to hunt down the legendary Headless Horseman. It was a made up story about a frightening, nogginless rider who galloped over the bridge of Sleepy Hollow one night on a ferocious stallion, searching for a head to set upon his empty, bloody stump. Ick.

But the tourists would not find even a whiff of the ghostly horseman in this particular town. They would always leave disappointed. They had come to the wrong Sleepy Hollow. Sleepy Hollow, Massachusetts was hundreds of miles from the town they were really looking for. It was actually Sleepy Hollow, *New York* they wanted. That was where author Washington Irving's famous story of the headless horseman took place.

1

Of course, the tourists were very sad when they learned the truth, and the town was losing business as word on Facebook spread. It was a lose-lose situation. So when Maximus Kligore was elected mayor, the first thing he did was to put a restoration program together to transform Sleepy Hollow into "Spooky Town."

He proclaimed every day Halloween night, and the scary transformation began. Rumor had it that the real reason behind the restoration was that Kligore had sold Sleepy Hollow's soul in exchange for some dark magic for himself. Whatever, Kligore's evil deal with the dark side worked. Sleepy Hollow's Halloween nightmare began making more money than anyone ever dreamed. Spooky Town became one of the country's most popular tourist towns.

The town even erected a statue of the Headless Horseman in the town square. The statue, made of bronze, stood a whopping fourteen feet high and had a steel ladder propped up against it. From Taiwan to Abu Dhabi, people came to the wrong town to have their pictures snapped on top of the horse, riding with the horseman who lost his head.

During Mayor Kligore's Halloween restoration, one little antique store was renamed I. C. Dead People. A sundry shop on Elm Street was transformed into Nightmare on Elm Street. The garden tour became Spooky Tours. The harvest hayrides became Haunted Hayrides. A failing toy store was transformed into the popular Ghost Busters Shoppe. There was even a street renamed Magic Row, where spells, incantations, and magic tricks could be purchased.

All year long, the public school promoted scares. The wooden marquee in front of Sleepy Hollow Middle School read "Home of the Annual Scary Talent Contest."

Over the years, Sleepy Hollow's fortunes returned. Spooky became big business. The trademarked Headless Horseman Plush Doll, available in almost every store, was a sell-out at Halloween. Sleepy Hollow Cemetery was the resting place of some of American history's greatest thinkers and writers, from Henry David Thoreau to Nathaniel Hawthorne. To most tourists, it was now the place where the fake Headless Horseman was buried.

❧

Slish. Slash. What was that noise? Harry turned. Someone must be following him. But there was no one behind him. Harry was a few blocks from his house. The wind was so intense that it even rattled the picket fences lining the many homes on Walking Dead Lane.

Slish. Slash. There was that noise again. Normally, Harry Moon would be walking home from school with his buddies, Declan Dickinson, Bailey Wheeler, and Hao Jones, but he had stayed behind to practice for the big contest. He was alerted to the odd noise simply because it was out of the ordinary. It was not the knocking fence or the whipping branches. It was the sound of metal scraping against metal.

Slish. Slash. He wondered how anything could

see to follow him in this darkness, as the sky was dim and there were no street lamps on Walking Dead Lane.

Slish. Slash. As the sound of metal against metal grew closer, Harry walked faster. His backpack slammed against his shoulders. He picked up speed, but so did the sound. As the wind whipped at the branches, Harry ran. But his legs were short, and the follower's legs were not.

As if by magic, Titus Kligore was suddenly standing across from Harry Moon at the intersection of Nightingale Lane and Walking Dead Lane. Harry huffed and puffed as Titus stood, stoic. Titus was as steady and massive as the bronze Headless Horseman.

"Get out of my way!" yelled Harry. He tried to run around Titus. Titus leaned to his side, blocking his path. Harry went to the right. Again, Titus stopped him with his girth.

Slish. Slash. Harry looked down at the sound of metal sliding across metal. Even in the dim light, he could see the shine of the

11

shears in Titus's hands. He opened and closed them. These were not paper or sewing scissors. They were *shears*—the kind used on farms to cut the wool off of sheep.

"What are you doing?"

"I've come to give you a trim," Titus said. His voice was gruff and menacing.

"Why would you want to do that?"

"Isn't your name Harry?"

"What of it?" Harry said, trying to dodge Titus.

"Well, I have come to give your Harry Moon-butt a haircut," replied Titus.

"No way!" Harry cried, wiggling in Titus's grasp.

For as long as he could remember, Harry had suffered indignities with the double meaning of his name. He didn't even realize there was a problem with his name until he was eleven. A bus filled with the Sleepy Hollow Booster Club had driven past Harry and his buddies. It was headed to a football game. On that autumn day, several of the high school seniors pulled down their pants and stuck their naked butts through the open windows.

"Hey, boys!" shouted the pranksters in the bus. Harry and his sixth-grade friends gawked. "Here's something to look forward to!"

Harry and his friends laughed until their sides split. They did not fully understand what was going on. They laughed, anyway, as they watched the flank of bare rear ends waving from the windows.

Declan Dickinson, the tech-geek in the group, kept his cool. "What do we have to look forward to?" he shouted to the busload of boosters.

"Your pink fannies becoming hairy moons, that's what!" a rowdy booster shouted back.

"What do you think that freak show was all

13

about?" asked Harry as he kicked at some fallen leaves.

"Just stupid fools, making a scene in the little suburb of Sleepy Hollow is all," answered Hao Jones. He was the most mild-mannered of the guys.

"Eww, pretty nasty!" added Bailey.

"That's adulthood for you," said Harry, with a sigh. "I never wanna grow up and be like those silly fools."

"Yeah. Well, they seem to be calling for you, Harry Moon, to become a fool with them," said Declan with some snideness in his voice.

"Whaddaya mean?" Harry inquired.

"They seem to know your name, 'Harry Moon.'"

"They were referring to their naked butts, not to me."

"I guess it's the same. I mean 'hairy moon' or 'Harry Moon'?" said Bailey. "Sounds like they are one and the same to me. That's just some real nasty, ugly bare-butt business."

"Ah, get outta here," said Harry. "That was moonin'. Everyone who is sophisticated knows about moonin'."

"Yeah, well, now that I am sophisticated and know of such things," said Bailey as he slithered his eyes over his friend, "I can't unsee that. You have a hairy moon face."

15

"Me neither, Harry Moon," said Declan. "I can't unsee it, either!" He opened his mouth as if to gasp. Instead, he laughed hysterically, taking off after Bailey. The two of them jumped up and flicked the branches of the maple trees as they dashed. The autumn leaves fell from the branches.

"I don't mind hanging with you, Harry Moon," said Hao. "They just think they're funny, not mean. Don't worry. They'll get over their nonsense by breakfast."

Sure enough, Hao Jones was right. By the next day, with a new sun shining, as Harry walked to school, there were his buddies—Declan, Bailey, and Hao. They waited for him under the maple tree at the corner of Nightingale and Mayflower.

"Hey, man, we're sorry," said Declan. "We were just messing with you. We didn't mean it. We just thought it was funny—that's all."

16

"It is kind of funny," said Harry, "and kind of ironic too."

"How is it ironic?" asked Hao. He had spent the night on his cell phone, convincing his buddies they needed to apologize to Harry.

"It's ironic because I don't have a hairy rear."

"Yet," said Bailey. "Not yet."

They all laughed and "ewwed" at the thought as they walked down the sidewalk and away from the intersection. They were four friends. Bailey, Harry, and Declan had known one

another since daycare. Hao was the newbie when he moved to town in the third grade. "Are you black or Asian or Indian or what?" asked Bailey when Hao came into the third grade classroom.

"I'm a little bit of everything. Just call me

'world child.' That's who I am," replied Hao. Hao needed to say no more. Harry and his friends liked him immediately.

They called themselves the Good Mischief Team, although they did not always do good. They even had secret Good Mischief meetings in the tree house in the Moon backyard. And as much as Harry's sister protested, she was not invited. She was not great at keeping secrets.

18

Now, it was night. Two years later. The wind howled. It was dark.

Slish. Slash. Titus towered over Harry. The clouds drifted over the butter-yellow moon. The shadow of the sheep shears fell over Harry's face.

"Either you are going to drop out of the talent show, or I am going to cut off your hair, Harry Moon-butt," threatened Titus. He leaned in and grabbed a chunk of Harry's hair.

Titus pulled Harry off the ground by his hair. Harry screamed in pain. *Slish. Slash.* The sheers swished in Titus's hands. Harry

managed to struggle loose but not before Titus chopped off a small clump of Harry's hair. Harry stumbled and fell to the sidewalk. As Titus threw the hair onto the ground, Harry Moon scrambled to his feet and ran for his life.

Titus turned and chased after him. Pulling his backpack from his shoulders, Harry swung it backward at Titus's big head. He knocked Titus to the ground.

"I'll get the rest of your hair later," Titus said through gritted teeth.

Harry ran as fast as his short stride could carry him. Before Titus could rise again, Harry was already down the street, disappearing into the green of his own front yard.

THE SLEEPY HOLLOW MAGIC SHOPPE

"You gotta let me change my name!" howled Harry.

Harry sat with his parents at the dinner table, facing his chicken and rice pilaf.

"No one is changing their name around

here," said John Moon, Harry's father.

"Trust me, Harry, I have tried," said his ten-year-old sister, Honey Moon. Honey had straight, chestnut-colored hair. Her bright, green eyes shone beneath an always-worried brow. "Every time I turn around, someone in class is making a crack about me kissing or making out."

"At least they're not cutting your hair off," growled Harry, as he grabbed at his missing hair. "Look, Titus Kligore cut my hair."

"No one will notice," said Honey unhelpfully. "You never comb it, so who will ever know? It looks just fine. Be happy your name isn't Honey or Harvest."

Honey looked over at her little brother, Harvest Moon, as he sat in a booster chair at the table.

"Wha' wrong wif my name?" asked Harvest, as he plopped his hands into the apple sauce.

"It's a lovely name," said Harry's mom, Mary Moon. "It's like a wonderful poem."

"I need to legally change my name to George or Milo!" Harry pleaded. "And I need to do it before Saturday! That's the night of the talent show." Harry opened his arms as if imagining a dream. "Can't you see it, Dad? Can't you see it, Mom? 'And now . . . ladies and gentlemen . . . from Nightingale Lane, presenting his amazing magic, the one and only, Milo Moon!' That sounds awesome, don't you think?"

"No, I do not think so," said his dad. "We Moons do not back down just because of some little adversity."

"Little adversity?" Harry replied. "I was attacked with sheep shears!"

"How many times have we discussed your name?" John said with a kind, but firm, manner. "You were named after Harrold Runyon, and you will carry his name with the same nobility as he carried it."

"Yes, sir," said Harry glumly.

"You just have to rise above name-calling," said John.

Harry knew it was going to be another losing battle. During the Iraq War, his dad's best army buddy was a man named Harrold Runyon. Harrold was a gregarious, gum-chewing, wise-

cracking, got-your-back kind of fellow. From the age of fourteen, Harrold worked summers as a lifeguard at the Leisure Time Pool in Kansas City, Missouri. That's what Harrold did. He saved scrawny girls and boys from drowning.

When he was eighteen, Harry Runyon saved John from dying too. In Iraq, he took a bullet in the heart for his buddy. John grieved for his army friend, threw the first shovel of dirt over his coffin in Missouri, and vowed that he would keep his friend's memory alive. So when John and Mary Moon had their first child, they named the boy Harrold in honor of John's friend who gave his life so that Harry's dad might live.

"Let's not forget excellence, dear," added Mary Moon.

"What do you mean, Mom?" asked Harry, swallowing the last of his rice pilaf.

"Titus Kligore is worried about you," replied his mom.

"Worried about me? He's a beast!" said Harry.

"He wouldn't be picking on you if he wasn't driven by fear. Don't try and punch him out in the school yard," explained Mary. "Nothing good can come of that. Instead, punch him out by being great at the talent show."

"But, Mom, how can Harry do that, when he's not so excellent himself?" said Honey in her matter-of-fact way.

"Be quiet!" Harry shouted at Honey.

"Truth is hard," Honey added. "Let's face it, Harry. You need better tricks."

Harry did not like his sister. He loved her, but he didn't like her. She was almost always right. He didn't like that either. This time, she was all-the-way right. If he was going to beat the bully, Titus Kligore, with excellence, he needed better tricks.

Harry had a good excuse to look for some superior magic tricks. Half Moon, the family dog, had chewed up Harry's white fiberglass wand, so Harry had decided he was ready for the deep magic. He had been studying magic for some time. Now, he knew he was ready to take the next step. Harry had some money saved from the magic shows he performed at kids' birthday parties, so he had peeled off a few dollars from his savings for the purchase. Harry had been waiting for the right time, and now, with the Scary Talent Show approaching fast, he knew it was time to head to Magic Row.

Mary did not like the idea of Harry wandering around on Magic Row or Conical Hat Avenue on his own. He was only in eighth grade. But, long ago, she had what appeared to be a chance meeting with an eccentric man in the Boston Common. Back then, Harry was still a baby in a stroller. The man had foretold that Mary and John Moon would move to Sleepy Hollow.

Sure enough, after three years in Boston, the Moon family relocated to a lovely house on Nightingale Lane, which Mary had inherited from her great-aunt. This eccentric man had also told Mary that Harry Moon was a child born to a special fate. The future of not only Sleepy Hollow but the world hung in the balance. Over time, Mary Moon had resigned herself to the knowledge that Harry would sometimes need to go places and do things before she was ready to let him.

Of all the stores on Magic Row, Harry was especially taken with the store with the most innocuous name—The Sleepy Hollow Magic Shoppe. It was not so much because of the shop windows, which had the latest gimmicks, but the proprietor within.

This man had wise eyes so bright they twinkled even at a distance. Over the years, this eccentric man had trained Harry. When Harry had excitedly introduced his mom to his mentor, Mary was aghast when she realized the proprietor of the magic store was the same man who had mysteriously appeared to her in Boston so many years earlier. "Nothing, Mary Moon, is by chance. Luck does not exist," the owner of the Sleepy Hollow Magic Shoppe had said when they met again in his magic store.

This man, this wizard, went by the name of Samson Dupree. Mary Moon and John Moon accepted this teacher as a guardian, of sorts, to Harry. Samson helped Harry to wonder and think and dream about life and the deep magic.

Harry would lie on his bed, stare at the ceiling, and wonder—was all magic an illusion? After all, superhero stories, video games, and movies were phony. Was magic true?

For sure, his mother didn't like magic very much. When Harry bought a simple magic starter kit, she tolerated it, but she did not like it. No, not one bit. But she also knew that it was his destiny.

One day, while bringing the fresh-pressed laundry into her son's room, Mary noticed a poster of a life-sized man tacked to Harry's bedroom wall.

"Harry, what is Tarzan doing on this newly stenciled wall?"

"That's not Tarzan."

"Sure it is, honey. I mean—look at him. He's in a loincloth, he's half naked, and he's leaning over like an animal grunting . . ."

"That's Elvis Gold, Mom. He is summoning the magic. Don't you see those chains around him? He's busting them with his power."

31

"Power? The only true power comes from Heaven above," said Mary, shaking her head.

"Mom, you know that, and I know that. Elvis Gold doesn't have real power. He is an illusionist. He is an expert at the sleight of hand."

"How can he hide his hand? There's nowhere to put it! He is dressed like a caveman in a loincloth!"

Mary sighed as she put Harry's clean

clothes in the drawers of his oak dresser.

"That's the point, Mom. He's really good. He is doing the sleight of hand without anything hiding the sleight. He is that good. He is my hero."

"Hero? Elvis Gold is your hero? Why can't you be like the other boys? Mark Rutherford has a poster of Abraham Lincoln in his bedroom. But my son? Nooo. He has Elvis Gold!"

Once Mary finished, she left his room like she often did—shaking her head. Of course, Mary loved Harry and, likewise, Harry loved his mom. At times, they frustrated one another.

It was times like this when Mary Moon remembered the words of Samson Dupree. "Do not fear, Mary," Samson had said.

☙

The town square was jumping the next afternoon. It was just a few days before Halloween. This was high season in Sleepy Hollow.

Busloads of tourists and consumers filled the parking lots. Everyone was out buying their last-minute costumes and trick-or-treat decorations for their Halloween parties.

As there was no practice that afternoon for the talent show, Harry decided it was time to finally get the wand. "Any of you guys want to come with me?" Harry asked his friends. Declan, Hao, and Bailey bowed out in favor of playing Declan's new video game.

33

Heading to the square, Harry could not believe the line at the Headless Horseman statue. There had to be a hundred people waiting to climb the ladder and perch on the saddle for their photo opportunity. "'Tis the season," Harry muttered under his breath, shaking his head.

As Harry walked across the town green, he looked at Magic Row. Chillie Willies was busy, and so was Twilight, the shop named after the vampire books and movies. But the Sleepy Hollow Magic Shoppe seemed to be empty. *Maybe it's just not spooky enough*, Harry thought as he stopped and stared at his favorite store from a distance.

The shop had cheery yellow-and-red striped awnings, which shaded two windows. From far away, two sparkling eyes seemed to look out from beneath the sunny eyelids. Even from this distance, Harry could hear the music of the door chimes, even before he opened the door.

The movement of the shoppers walking through the square faded as Harry approached the shop. As he walked, it seemed that time itself had stopped and there was no rush to anything. It was always that way when Harry sought the deep magic from his mentor, Samson Dupree. Now, it was time. *Now, I am ready. It's time for THE WAND.*

Suddenly, a black town car came out of nowhere. It seemed to speed up as it rumbled toward him. It veered across the road. Harry leaped to the sidewalk as the car went careening by, missing him by just inches.

Harry lay crumpled on the sidewalk. He rolled over and looked at the menacing town car as it reeled away. The frame on the license plate read "We Drive By Night." Harry Moon was not a stranger to these dark town cars. They always seemed to be lurking about, following him, ever since he was just a child.

He brushed off his pants and looked toward the shop. In the eyes of the window, he saw his magic teacher, the old man, Samson Dupree. A golden crown perched on his head, Samson, standing on a stepladder, unpacked boxes and stacked new inventory on the shelves.

35

As Harry laid eyes upon Samson, the door to the Sleepy Hollow Magic Shoppe swung wide all by itself. He loved that. He never understood exactly how that happened. The chime attached to the door rang sweetly. Harry smiled at the familiar tune. It always made him feel like a kid coming home.

Anything that a young magician could ever want stood on the racks and shelves of the store—capes, top hats, contraptions, puzzles, and scarves. Magic 8 Balls hung in nets from the ceiling.

There were the famous wizards of olde sitting royally on a marble shelf at the top of the store. Dumbledore, Gandalf, and of course, Merlin sat in majestic bronze. Their faces were wise and kindly. Once in a while, on other visits to the shop, Harry felt they looked directly at him. But Harry was not scared by such looks. Here in the Sleepy Hollow Magic Shoppe, Harry felt understood. Here, Harry felt loved.

36

"Samson . . . I am ready for the deep magic."

As Harry spoke, the man on the stepladder turned. He wore a plastic, golden crown on his head. A purple cape flowed from his shoulders. Upon his feet were two red slippers as bright a red as any polished orchard apple. When his periwinkle eyes affixed their gaze upon Harry, Samson beamed with a most beneficent smile. It was so friendly, so *other*, surely that smile could coax even the wildest wood beast into happy playfulness.

They had a certain patter down between

or gal? *Is what I am doing truthful, pure, of goodwill, and of service to all?*

"Yes!" Harry replied, enthusiastically.

"Then what can I do but trust you, my friend?" said Samson with a smile.

"Bottom line, I need better tricks!" Harry replied.

Samson flinched just a tad as Harry spoke. Then Samson moved from behind the counter and stood in front of the boy. Samson held up his right arm, caped in purple. He flashed his arm in front of Harry's face. *Swish!* Harry knew what this was. This was the famous *one arm appear* or the *one arm vanish*, depending on the circumstance.

As the right arm went in front of the left arm, the viewer's eyes affixed to the moving arm. *Swish!* Once the right arm was out of view—*pa-pow*—before the viewer was an object in the magician's hand.

them. Samson was the teacher of magic. He constantly wanted to reinforce the idea that no true magician could do anything without discipline and study of the practice. "You have studied my grimoire?" asked Samson, his eyes gleaming. The grimoire was a textbook of magic.

"I have," said Harry with a smile.

"You have learned the teachings of the Great Magician?"

37

"You know it," Harry replied.

"Do you honestly believe you are fully prepared for the wand, Harry?" asked Samson. He gently backed his way down the ladder.

In that moment, Harry wondered if he really was. Samson had never really asked him that question before. Was he prepared or did he just want to beat the pants off of Titus Kligore? Just like his dad always did when trying to make a decision, had he really answered the four questions that marked any standup guy

In this case, Harry looked to Samson's left hand. There in his palm were three fantastic wands. Each was made of wood and varnished into a sparkling shine. Immediately, Harry muscled up. He brought his mind, heart, body, and soul into focus. He knew this was a test from Samson Dupree. Harry understood

from his readings of the grimoire that life held many tests. *Sure, Samson trusts me, but do I really know my stuff? I hope so.*

"You know, of course, this wand is not one you can purchase from an *Elvis Gold Magic Kit*," said Samson. Harry walked toward Samson almost reverently. He looked at the wands.

"This is the wand that pulls the energy of the cosmos?"

"*One* of them does," said Samson. "Choose it."

"Can I inspect them?" Harry asked.

"I would think you would have to!" Samson said with a chortle. "Otherwise, how would you know, Harry Moon?"

Harry had been coming to the store as long as he could remember. Yes, he loved it. Yes, this place was home. But he did not like the tests very much, even though he knew tests were part of life. He always worried that he would fail them. "Have courage, my friend," Samson often said.

Plucking the middle wand from Samson's hand, Harry rolled it in his fingers. He brought it to his nose and sniffed it like a guy sniffed a cigar. "So this one has the charm to bring together the power of the moon and the sun and gathers the power of the wind?"

"*One* of them does," said Samson. "Two of them don't."

41

Harry placed the polished wand on the counter. It was slightly lighter in tone than the two that still rested in Samson's palm.

"Why have you discarded it?" said Samson.

"That wand is made of holly wood. Holly does not have the power to wield *Sanctum Vinculum*. That kind of wood is used for table tricks."

Samson raised his left eyebrow. He nodded and smiled. "Very good."

Harry looked at the old man with the stealthiest eyes that any thirteen-year-old could ever muster. The old man's sparkle congealed into one powerful light as he stared with both eyes at little Harry Moon.

"So, Harry, which wand will it be?" Samson asked. He held the two pieces of wood in his palm. The sun slanted through the window. A sunbeam shone on the two wands.

42

Harry drew the second wand from Samson's hand and rolled it, once again, with his fingers. He brought it to his face. His nostrils did not like the smell. His face grimaced. "Ew," Harry said as he pulled the wand from his puckering nose.

"This wand is from the yew tree. The tree of death. It is bitter. It is used for black magic. I am surprised you even sell it here," said Harry.

"Who says I sell it? I am using it for your choosing test. No one should have it," replied Samson.

The old wizard opened his empty right

hand and directed its power toward the wand made of yew that Harry held. As he did, the wand flashed with fire. Harry dropped the burning wand from his fingers. The wand magically hovered in midair as the flames consumed it. Then the ash floated like autumn leaves to the floor.

"Answer this riddle," Samson said.

"Hit me up." Harry stared at the single wand that now rested in Samson's hand.

43

"What is the greatest gift we have?"

"Life," Harry replied.

"Beyond that. What is the greatest gift in life?" Samson asked with excitement.

"The ability to choose," Harry said.

"Exactly!" said Samson. "And why are you choosing this final wand?" Harry carefully looked at the wand in Samson's hand before he gave his assessment. He knew in his heart it was the wand.

"It comes from the Tree of Life. I know it is made from the almond branch for as I studied it, I saw that this branch once held the flowers and nuts of an almond. Just like the magic staff made of almond wood that Moses used to lead his people out of Egypt."

"Very good, my Harry. You did not choose the illusion of the holly wood nor the poison of the yew. You chose well. You have chosen right. You should know from your studies that with this powerful and ancient wand comes great responsibility. You must watch carefully. Others shall want it and try to take it from you."

With that, Samson turned his palm over, and the wand dropped in midair. It floated like a little cloud in the middle of the Sleepy Hollow Magic Shoppe.

"It shall come to know your voice. It shall come by your calling."

Harry watched the shiny stick of wood

suspended in air. "Does it have a name?"

"Wand."

"Come here, boy. Come on, Wand."

"It's not a dog. It's a wand."

"That's right," replied Harry. His face flushed red with embarrassment. He opened his hand and said in a soft, coaxing voice. "Come to me, Wand."

The wand glided through the air, and Harry grasped it in his hand. It felt good in his fingers as if it had always belonged there.

"So I have power now?" Harry asked, squeezing the wand between his fingertips, looking for a familiar grip like the handshake of a friend.

"You have always had power. Everyone has power, Harry. But now you can access even more force. This wand is a gatherer of vast physical and spiritual forces. Never forget, Harry Moon, all magic stems from the deep mystery of the Great Magician. In life, there are those that shall abuse it and misuse it. The deep magic shall be there for you. But you are its master."

Suddenly, he was frightened. "Samson, do you think I am really ready?"

"I shall send a helper to you, Harry. He shall guide you and encourage you with your powers through Wand."

"Who is that?"

"You'll know soon enough. Like me, you are a traveler, Harry. A tourist goes to a place and sees with his eyes. A traveler? He goes to a place and sees with his soul. Look through your soul, and he shall come through a most friendly giver."

SARAH SINCLAIR

It was at the talent show rehearsal the next day that Harry's magic started. Samson Dupree was right. There was deep magic in that wand. Harry had just pulled the almond wand out of his backpack. When he looked up, there she was. Sarah Sinclair—his former babysitter. The love of his life. She was a junior at Sleepy Hollow High School.

When Harry picked up the wand, Sarah Sinclair came out of the shadow of the auditorium and onto the rehearsal stage. She seemed giddy—as if something was about to happen—as if Harry Moon was in for a surprise.

48

"Sarah," exclaimed Harry, "what are you doing here?"

"I've come for rehearsal. Miss Pryor phoned me and said that, as long as I only assisted, I could help you out."

That is the best magic possible, Harry thought, practically standing on his tiptoes on the stage. That past summer, Sarah, dressed in the bangles and scarves of a genie, had been Harry's assistant in the summer magic shows he held in his backyard. Harry and Sarah had made a dynamic team. She was the girl in the box who Harry sawed in two. She was the keeper of the magic scarves and the top hat.

Sarah giggled backstage in the middle school auditorium. "Okay," she said, "I have something for you."

Harry looked at Sarah, thinking how beautiful she was. She was running in place with excitement, her saddle shoes doing a tap dance on the stage floor. Her cheeks were flushed.

"Now, close your eyes," she said. He did. "Close them good and tight, and put your hands over your eyes."

Clamping his eyes shut and standing steady, Harry was ready. "Hit me up."

"I am not very good at this," Sarah said in a delightful breathlessness, "but hold on just a second. I will be ready."

Harry could hear commotion in the background. He sensed his top hat moving off his magic table.

"Are you ready?" he asked.

"Just one more second," she replied as more noise leaked into his ears. "Okay . . . NOW!"

When he pulled his palms away, there was the love of his heart, Sarah Sinclair, standing in a green cardigan, holding his empty, black top hat in her hands.

"Now, for the fun part," she said. "Don't laugh! I'm not good at this like you! Hocus pocus, razz-a-matazz, and all that jazz!"

Her sweet incantation finished, Sarah reached into the hat and pulled out the most beauteous bunny Harry had ever seen.

He was a lop-eared, Harlequin rabbit. He was all white and gray, except for a spotted face and ears that were as inky black as Harry's hair. The rabbit looked like he had gotten hit by a clown pie with ink filling.

Sarah almost screamed with joy as she saw Harry's eyes go wide.

"Oh wow!" Harry exclaimed as he reached out with the hands of a sleepwalker toward the rabbit. "A real bunny!"

"Harry Moon!" she cried with jubilance. "Meet your new rabbit!"

"So beautiful," he whispered as he buried both of his hands in the rabbit's soft fur.

Sarah beamed her brightest smile, knowing that her gift was warmly received. She handed the huge rabbit to Harry. He clutched the rabbit to his chest and rubbed him under his chin.

"Hello, I'm going to call you Rabbit," Harry said as he hugged the warm bunny. Harry gazed at Sarah with all the sweetness of his heart. "Thank you! How did you ever afford him?"

"It was nothing, really, Harry . . . anything for my wonderful magician. I visited your friend at the Sleepy Hollow Magic Shoppe and told him I wanted to get you a real, live bunny for

51

your tricks."

She smiled. "He said this was a very special rabbit. It would bring you some very special magic. That's pretty cool, huh? And don't you worry, Harry. Titus Kligore has nothing on you."

Obviously, word had gotten back to Sarah about Titus bullying him.

52

Sarah saw that Harry was going to cry. She grabbed him and the rabbit, hugging them quickly as if to squeeze the tears from his eyes. They had a rehearsal to do.

"Should we use Rabbit in the show this Saturday?" Harry asked.

"Of course! Let everyone see him," Sarah replied.

"Shall we rehearse?" asked Harry.

So Harry, Sarah, and Rabbit got to work and refined the performance for Saturday night.

RABBIT

"Where's the new magic trick?" Honey Moon said when she burst into Harry's bedroom to ask for some help with math homework.

"Isn't Rabbit cool?" asked Harry as he

rubbed the black-and-white fur of Rabbit's neck. Rabbit and Harry were sitting on the bed.

"He's so cool that he's not even there," replied Honey Moon.

"Whaddaya mean?" asked Harry. "You can't see Rabbit?"

"When I told you to get a new magic trick, I didn't mean for you to get crazy."

"Huh?" said Harry as he looked over at the big bunny, larger than life, his face speckled in the black-and-white marks of the Harlequin.

"There's no rabbit anywhere, Har-rold," stated Honey Moon as she pulled on her hair.

All of a sudden, Rabbit spoke to Harry. "What do you want from me?" asked Rabbit. "Most people can't see me, so you have to put me into a trick and then they will know."

Harry looked sideways at Rabbit, surprised that he could talk.

"Huh? What do you mean?" Harry asked.

"Let Honey pull me out of the hat. In the trick, there I'll be!"

Harry ran over to his desk and picked his top hat up from the chair. He sat the hat on the bed. He picked up Rabbit and gently stuffed him into the hat.

Harry held the hat out and showed the inside to Honey.

"Empty . . . right?

"Empty as your head," scoffed Honey, rolling her eyes at her older brother. "I don't even know why I asked you to help me with my math."

"So, with one 'abracadabra,'" said Harry, "I am going to ask you to reach inside the hat and pull out Rabbit."

"You got it," she replied.

Harry held the top hat in his hand and

55

took his new almond-wood wand and waved it over the black top hat.

"A B R A C A D A B R A!" Harry said. "Come forward, Rabbit!"

Harry held out the top hat. "All right, Honey. You do it. Stick your hand in the hat and pull out the rabbit."

Honey rolled her eyes a second time. With a smirk on her face, she walked over to Harry and the top hat. With her right hand, she reached in. "You are an idiot, Har-rold."

"Ha! Of course! NOTHING! " she said as her fingers flitted against the empty insides of the hat.

"Reach farther!" said Harry in a commanding voice.

Honey stretched her arm into the hat until it had almost disappeared. "What the heck?" she asked, feeling something, anything. And then she screamed.

As she pulled her hand out, there was Rabbit. First his lop ears and his eyes—and then there was more of him as she pulled him completely from the hat. In fact, Rabbit was so large that Honey had to scoop his haunches into her left hand to prop him up in her arms.

"Wow," she said. "That is pretty amazing. I have no idea how you did that. He is heavy! What's his name?"

"Rabbit," Harry replied.

"Good name," she said. "How much does he weigh?"

"I don't know," said Harry.

Holding Rabbit in both hands, Honey struggled to open the bedroom door.

Harry followed after Honey as she marched through the upstairs hallway of the house into their parents' bedroom.

Their mom was at the sink brushing her teeth as Honey came into the bathroom and put Rabbit on the scale.

Mary looked down to see her daughter kneeling in front of the scale.

"What are you doing, Honey?" asked Mary.

"She's weighing Rabbit," Harry explained.

"I see," Mary said. But, of course, at this

point, she saw absolutely nothing.

"Wow!" said Honey, as the full weight of Rabbit hit the scale and the needle jumped and steadied. "Nine-and-a-half pounds!"

"That's more than I expected," admitted Harry, shaking his head.

"And why exactly are you weighing, what did you say, the rabbit?" asked their mom.

59

"We need to make sure we have a big enough hat," said Honey. "He can't be breaking the top hat on Saturday night with his size. It would ruin the trick."

"Of course," replied Mary as she continued to brush her teeth.

When they returned to Harry's bedroom, Honey had forgotten all about her math, but somehow, she now knew the answers.

"I have to hand it to you, Harry."

"Hand what to me, Honey?"

"When I said to get better tricks, you came through—big time."

Later that night, after he said his prayers, Harry climbed into his bed, and Rabbit lay down at the foot of it.

As usual, Harry stared up at the ceiling before he fell off to sleep. But now, he could feel the warmth of Rabbit at his toes.

"Rabbit?"

"Yes, Harry."

"How does it all work?" he asked.

"How does what work?"

"You."

"Well. I'm rather like goodness . . . good things like kindness and gentleness and self-control."

"How's that?"

"Just because you can't see them doesn't mean that they don't exist."

"Uh huh."

"Remember, my human friend, the most important things in life cannot be seen."

61

WAND

There were twelve acts competing for
the top prize on Scary Talent Night.
As was the tradition, the show always
went through a complete dress rehearsal
on the night before the Saturday show. The
order of the contestants was always decided

by drawing numbers from a hat.

As the draw of numbers would have it, the show would begin with a bang—Titus Kligore's Maniacs were first up. The employees at Chillie Willies had outdone themselves in building the most elaborate and authentic set and costumes for Titus and his friends. Their music was hot and dynamic. Besides all that, since they were athletes, their coordination was good.

64

Harry and Sarah sat with the other acts in the front seats of the auditorium. Her clipboard at the ready, Miss Pryor ran through the rehearsal with the precision of a well-tested operating system.

All Harry could think of was what his mom had said: "Beat him with excellence."

Sitting in the front row of the auditorium, Harry watched the Maniacs. Titus was Freddie. He was the lead singer. Jason, Jigsaw, and the Werewolf sang backup. They danced to the song. The dance seemed almost tribal. Harry wondered how he could ever beat these bullies with excellence.

"Where there's a will, there's a way," said Rabbit.

"Huh?" asked Harry. "You can read my mind?"

"For heaven's sake, Harry. There are no secrets between you and me. Besides, we should be concentrating on what we can do, not on what they can do."

"You're right, Rabbit," said Harry as he looked at the spectacular set that Kligore money had put together. "It's just not fair," muttered Harry, dangling his thrift shop top hat from his fingertips.

"Who said that life was fair? We're talking about excellence!" reminded Rabbit.

"Okay, okay," Harry said as he watched, mesmerized. The Maniacs even had robotic trees and fences that moved back and forth thanks to a custom computer program, courtesy of Chillie Willies. When the Maniacs were finished with "Let's Get Hysterical," they sat down at the front of the auditorium with the rest of the contestants.

As Titus Kligore walked down the aisle, he made sure to lay his hand on Harry's head and made a cutting gesture with his fingers like scissor blades.

"Next time I'm gonna take it off from the neck up." Titus hissed with a laugh. Harry sighed.

"That's enough, Titus Kligore," Miss Pryor shouted. She was not at all intimidated by Titus, even though he was a head taller than her. She was a teacher, after all.

The protocol for the contest was to be polite, demonstrating good sportsmanship. Anyone not adhering to the rules would be suspended from the show. Harry was not about to be a Titus snitch because no one liked snitches at Sleepy Hollow Middle School. Sometimes a snitch was thought to be even worse than a bully.

Through the course of the rehearsal, Titus and his Maniacs would hoot and holler when an act would finish, especially the weaker acts like Carrie Taylor with her Casper song or Tanner Douglas and his twin sisters with Zombie Mash.

When Harry and Sarah arrived on stage as the last act, Titus stood up before they could get a word out. Titus shouted, "Foul! Foul! Cheater! That's no fair, Moon!"

"Titus, sit down!" shouted Miss Pryor from the side of the stage.

"But, Miss Pryor, Sarah Sinclair is a *junior*," Titus answered. "She should not even *be* here!"

Miss Pryor, knowing that Titus complained about everything, was prepared. With a sigh, she pulled the talent show manual from her clipboard and read from Rule Four, Section G.

"Up to three adults can assist the participant in preparing for or exhibiting in the show on or off stage. They can only assist and are forbidden from participating in the act, i.e. singing, dancing, the playing of an instrument, juggling, or performing magic." She peered out over the top of the clipboard and simply said, "Sarah Sinclair is an adult, and she is assisting only. Now, sit down, Titus!"

Titus slouched down in his auditorium chair as Sarah perked up with the mention of being an adult. With a mature confidence previously unknown to her, Sarah twirled about the stage. She was dressed as a genie, her pink veils falling by her side.

Harry Moon's Amazing Magic Show began with the trademark tipping of his black top hat to the audience.

"He's such a geek! He looks like Mr. Do-Not-Pass-Go from the Monopoly Game," Titus whispered to his buddy, Finn Johnson. "BORING!" He grunted loud enough for everyone to hear.

Harry pulled scarves out of the air as Sarah delicately attached them to her costume. There were so many of them that Sarah was positively afloat with the colors.

"She looks like Cotton Candy Big Foot." Titus sneered as his pals laughed at his observation. Harry Moon's act was good, as always, but there were no new tricks—not yet.

"Can you tell me, Miss Sinclair," asked Harry, "is this hat empty?" He showed her his top hat.

With her wrists jingling with the golden bangles, Sarah reached into the hat.

"Why, it is, Mr. Moon!" she exclaimed in a firm voice.

69

"And now I will wave my wand over the hat," said Harry in his red cape and shiny shoes. "This wand is made of almond wood— the same almond wood that, in ancient times, made frogs rain from the sky and seas part as the people left Egypt."

"What the heck?" said Titus. "The guy is blaspheming."

"What does blaspheming mean?" Finn asked.

Titus and Finn watched with the rest of the competitors as Harry ran the wand over the top hat, proclaiming, "A B R A C A D A B R A!"

With Sarah holding the hat, Harry reached inside and pulled out the lop ears of a black-and-white rabbit. Harry kept pulling as Sarah held the hat. As the Harlequin rabbit was slowly revealed, the rabbit seemed almost as big as Harry. The contestants broke into applause, shaking their heads. There was no possible way that a bunny that size could fit into that small top hat.

Rabbit stood on his haunches. He took a bow to the audience, nodding to their applause.

In anger, Titus rose to his feet. "What the heck?" said Titus to Finn. "That whole rabbit thing is totally not fair! Whoever saw an animal make a bow like that? Must be a robot or something. Moon is a stinkin' cheater."

Even Miss Pryor had a look of shock on her face, as the rabbit seemed almost anthropomorphic.

"Now," said Rabbit in a soft voice to be heard only by Harry, "take the wand and tell me to rise."

"What? This isn't in the skit," Harry whispered out of the side of his mouth, all the while smiling at his audience.

"You, yourself, said you have a wand that makes frogs rain. Let's get on with it."

At the risk of complete embarrassment, Harry waved his almond-wood wand over the top of the Harlequin. He commanded, "Rise, Rabbit!"

Immediately, Rabbit's lop ears stood up like telephone poles on either side of his head. Rabbit's front paws stretched up toward the rafters as if he were going for a swim. Then, as if the air around him took on the density of water, Rabbit began to make strokes with his front paws, and he was lifted off the stage. The rabbit swam higher into the air. Sarah spread her arms wide to the audience. She opened her mouth in awe.

The other contestants in the front rows watched as the Harlequin rabbit swam above Harry and Sarah on the stage. There were no strings or wires to be seen holding up the enchantment. Rabbit then floated onto his side and used his haunches to paddle so that he could wave like a beauty queen in a processional parade.

Sarah smiled and, through the side of her mouth, whispered to Harry, "Wow, Harry, that's pretty unbelievable. I think it's time to bring him down."

Harry looked up at the waving Rabbit. "Return, Rabbit!" he finally said. He planted an expression on his face to indicate "standard procedure."

Rabbit glided lightly downward like a party balloon losing its helium. On the table stood the black top hat. With great aplomb, Rabbit fell into the opening of the hat, pouring his black-and-white fur into the funnel of the hat as if he were milk being poured into a glass.

Once Rabbit had vanished, Sarah picked up the top hat from the table and demonstrated to the contestants that the hat was now empty. With a big smile, she turned and placed the hat on Harry's head. They both bowed and left the stage.

The other contestants erupted with applause, except for Titus, who had sunk into his chair with a huge frown on his face, thinking. His father was the owner of Chillie Willies. He was the mayor. If he did not win this silly middle school contest somehow, Titus would be disappointing his father. His father did not take disappointment well. Titus could not, under any circumstance, let his dad down. Titus would have to do something about Harry Moon and this new development. He clenched his fists, as did the other Maniacs, following their leader.

"Well, all right then," said Miss Pryor, obviously a little shaken by what she had just seen. She turned to a teacher's aide sitting next to her and silently mouthed the words, "What the heck was that?" Gaining her composure, Miss Pryor returned to the participants. "Thank you, contestants, for a most interesting rehearsal! I will see you all at six p.m. Saturday. It should be a very interesting show. Techies, please stay as I have a few notes."

Once they were at the back of the auditorium, Harry and Sarah stood quietly, trying to take it all in. Sarah's performance smile vanished.

"What just happened, Harry Moon?" she asked Harry.

Harry looked at her. He did not yet know what to say. He did not yet know if it was true. But somehow, between Wand and Rabbit, something unbelievable had just happened. His heart pounded against his ribs.

"What happened, Harry?" Sarah asked again. This time she was almost desperate. Harry could hardly get it out. But when he did, it was but one single word.

"Magic."

Some Bad Mischief

Harry walked home alone. A strong breeze blew through the trees, shaking the branches of their last leaves, making the little town of Sleepy Hollow ready for a spooky Halloween. Lightning crackled in the distance and thunder boomed overhead even though it had not started to rain. As Harry watched the dark horizon, the trees looked like walking skeletons heading to some unknown gathering of the dead.

But Harry Moon was not frightened. Even though this was the scene of Titus Kligore roughing him up the other night, he had his rabbit and his wand. He was still reeling from the deep magic that had swept through him. He thought about when Rabbit had sailed across the stage to great applause.

He took Wand out of his backpack as he walked with the invisible rabbit by his side. He turned his face upwards to the chestnut tree and waved his wand, shouting, "A B R A C A D A B R A!"

Upon this command, leaves shot out of the branches and the tree bloomed. Within moments, the tree was flush with shining chestnuts. Harry blinked as the chestnuts fell from the branches, raining down on the sidewalk and yard.

He looked over at a stone wall that surrounded the Meldrum's front yard. With a simple glance at three of the stones, Harry waved his wand again, but this time over the wall, saying, "A B R A CA D A B R A!"

With the incantation, the three stones shifted into three large pumpkins, which now sat on top of the wall. Harry smiled at the magic he had created. He thought a bit more and waved his wand again. The pumpkins became toothy jack-o'-lanterns with big eyes. When one of the orange lanterns winked at Harry, he freaked, dashing down the road.

Harry ran so fast that he did not notice the shadowy figure in front of him. He ran right into the menacing form, falling backward on his butt, rolling into the MacDougal's yard.

Looking up from the grass, Harry saw the large figure etched against the harvest moon. The buzz haircut and the lantern jaw could be no other—Titus Kligore!

"Give me that thing!" Titus ordered. His silhouette loomed in front of Harry.

"Give you what?" asked Harry, knowing full

well what Titus was talking about. Harry and Rabbit were both on the grass. Of course, Titus could not see Rabbit. He could only see the wand in Harry's hand.

"The wand thing," demanded Titus. "Give it!"

"It won't work for you. You're not a magician," said Harry as he clutched the almond wand to his chest.

"If it will work for you, it will work for me," insisted Titus, as he reached down to the ground. He grabbed Harry's neck in a vice grip with one hand. With his other hand, he pulled the wand from Harry's grasp.

"Now let's see just who the magician is around here," said Titus. He waved the wand at Harry. "Aberkeydabya," he said, "Turn this geek to dog crap!"

81

Titus waited. Harry remained on the ground.

"See?" said Harry, riled up. "It isn't going to work for you."

"Oh, it will work for me, little man," he sneered. "Don't you worry."

"I'm not worried!"

"Aberkeydabyou! Take Harry to jail!"

shouted Titus as he waved the wand again at the crumpled eighth grader at his feet. Titus made his command with great flare. His gestures, however, still did not succeed in changing Harry's locale from the MacDougal's front yard to the Sleepy Hollow Jail.

Angry, Titus took the wand in both hands and tried to break it in two like a Thanksgiving wishbone.

"Sorry, dude," Harry said. "You're too weak. You don't have the strength to break its power." Harry was right. With no success, Titus threw the wand across the MacDougal's lawn. With both hands, Titus lifted Harry up and pushed his back against an oak tree.

Titus was massive. It was hard for Harry to hold his own.

"So what will it be tonight, Harry Moon? I guess it won't be the wand. And it certainly won't be paper. I guess it will have to be scissors."

Slish. Slash. Out came the sheep shears. The blades shone in the moonlight. Harry called for his wand, but it did not obey. In his mind, he commanded it in every way he could, attempting to get the wand into his hand. He was just learning its magic, and Wand did not come.

At first, Harry thought Titus was so angry that he was going to punch the scissors into his eyes. Instead, the blades rose above his eyes, and Titus grabbed his hair. "This time I won't miss." *Slish. Slash. Slish. Slash.* Off it came in clumps. Several times the tips of the scissors clipped into his scalp, cutting him.

Once Titus was finished to his satisfaction, and Harry's hair was on the sidewalk, Titus looked at him and laughed.

"You look like my dog, Oink, when he gets shaved for the summer. Don't show yourself on stage or screen until it all grows back!"

Harry was seething, but he knew to stay quiet. He knew there was no point in riling Titus any further until there was something he could do about it.

Titus turned and walked back into the shadows. Harry scrambled across the lawn. He was on high alert as his eyes looked everywhere in the grass for the wand.

"Where are you, Wand? Where are you?" he said, crawling through the grass. But he seemed to be alone. Harry had even forgotten about Rabbit.

There, next to the sad, autumn flowerbed where Mrs. MacDougal had raised her prize-winning gardenia plants, was the wand.

As Harry reached for it, his fear gave way to a new-found courage. He called out to the shadows, "Not so fast, Kligore!" His voice was full of vengeance and anger.

As Harry took hold of the wand and stood, he saw Titus Kligore walking out of the darkness toward the small magician. "Now you'll see what the deep magic is all about!" Harry shouted. Never one to shrink from a dare, Titus walked toward Harry.

"I am going to lop your head off with a cut as clean as the Horseman in the square," said Harry. "Then I am going to hide your head so you can spend your lifetime looking for it!"

"Go ahead, Magic Man! Make my day!" Titus shouted. He laughed as he stood on the sidewalk, no longer in the shade of the trees, the moonlight shining on him.

Harry thrust his wand toward the bully. "A B R A C A D A B R A!" Harry shouted. "As I have said, hide his head!"

Titus waited for the magic, but nothing happened. He smirked at Harry. Undaunted, Harry tried again with more vengeful fever than before. "As I have said, HIDE HIS HEAD!"

"Hiding my head wouldn't mean much, little man. They say I don't have much of one to begin with." With that, Titus chuckled, shaking his head as he looked at Harry's hair. "My my, that boogie-man barber did a number on you. I suspect you won't be going anywhere for a while and certainly not to the talent show. Now, remember, that was the boogie man, not me—or I'll come sneaking by and cut up the rest of you."

With wand in hand and finished with his attempted bad mischief, Harry ran to the other side of the street. His backpack banged against his shoulders. Titus watched as Harry disappeared into the shadows. The bully was convinced that Harry would not be back. And he certainly would not show up for the Annual Scary Talent Show!

IMAGINE

As he approached his house, Harry noticed that only the front porch light was on. It was getting late. He walked to the door and looked into the foyer but saw no one. In the glass, he caught his reflection.

"Oh no!" he cried. He saw a scared kid

with chunky bits of hair sprouting from his head. Gone was the delightful, highly cultivated, spilled ink bottle of hair! In its place was the fur of a road kill. Harry rustled through his backpack for his ski cap and scrunched it over his hideous head, just in case his parents were lurking about.

He snuck quietly through the front door and tiptoed across the entryway. His father was on the landing, looking down the banister.

"There you are!" shouted his dad, a bright grin on his face. He was soon joined by Harry's mom, already in her nightgown and robe. "My son, the magician! The phone has been ringing off the hook!"

Hearing the commotion, Honey Moon, in her princess pajamas, came to the banister and poked her head through the rails so she could get a good look at her brother below. "And not just our cell phones," said Honey, "but the landline as well. Who calls on the landline anyway? Everyone was calling tonight!"

"Whaddaya mean?" he questioned, scrunching his hat down over his hair disaster.

"Everyone's talking about your magic at rehearsal and that you made a rabbit fly."

"I guess I did," Harry said, still unsure of how to talk about the amazing thing that happened during the rehearsal.

"I heard from Lila Davish," confided Honey. "Her sister is Casper in the show. She says you are a shoo-in to win tomorrow night. You are Lila's he-rooooooo!"

"Knock it off, Honey!" Harry shouted. "A guy can't just perform excellent magic without you making fun of it?"

"All right, all right. Come on, Harry!" said John, as he flopped down the stairs in his 1970s original *Star Trek* fuzzy slippers. "You and I are going to have a hot-fudge sundae to celebrate."

"I'll come too!" Honey chimed in.

"No, dear," Mary said. "Your father has something to discuss with Harry."

Honey nodded as if she understood. She stoically marched back to her room.

In the kitchen, John Moon went to work on the hot-fudge sundae. *Obviously, Dad has been lying in wait for me*, thought Harry. The hot fudge was already simmering on the stove. *This must be pretty bad.* Harry slumped on the stool at the kitchen island. He pulled his ski cap lower over his forehead.

"Aren't you hot?" his dad asked. "Don't you

want to take that hat off?"

"I feel a little chilled," Harry said. The last thing he wanted to do was admit Titus had cut his hair again, and this time he had completed the job. Indeed, he was telling the truth. His road-kill head was not used to so much empty space up there on his scalp. Harry and his dad made small talk as John pulled the perfectly rounded scoops of ice cream, already prepared, from the sub-zero freezer compartment.

91

"Harry, I hope you understand that the magic you perform on stage is sheer trickery," explained his dad. Harry could already tell that his dad's speech was as prepared as the scoops of ice cream.

"Trickery?" asked Harry.

"Illusion. You manipulate reality, but you're not changing it."

"Oh? Dad, have you seen my latest act? Where do you think the source of my magic comes from?" Harry asked.

"The same place your hero, Elvis Gold, gets it. He's very good."

"Oh, he is more than good, Dad. He is a genius."

"But, you do understand, Harry, that Elvis Gold is a big quack. His magic is not real." John doused the ice cream with hot fudge from the pan.

92

"You mean all smoke and mirrors?"

"Exactly, Harry. I know he is a terrific showman. But by definition, he is a fraud. He's not really doing any of it. Let's face it. In the end, Elvis Gold is one big phony. That's why they call him an illusionist. I just want you to realize that the stuff you read in those superhero comics is just fantasy. You are not really making rabbits fly in the air. This is all pretend."

"But is it possible, Dad, to have real magic? After all, we live and breathe because of the Great Magician," Harry replied. John handed

Harry the can of whipped cream. Harry was quick to spray both their sundaes with rapid-fire panache.

"There you go again, son. You know what Pastor McAdams says about that hooey. You talk about too many crazy ideas. Remember, you're from the little town of Sleepy Hollow, Massachusetts. Maybe it's best if you don't spend all your time on the Internet. It's filling your mind with all kinds of crazy, unrealistic stuff. This is precisely the point of my talk with you tonight, Harry. You need to be more sensible about things."

"Dad, it is not the Internet that is giving me such thoughts."

John placed cherries on top of the two sundaes. He slid one gorgeous sundae across the island to Harry and kept one for himself. John Moon did not like it when his son started to talk like this. He found, too often, that Harry seemed to be twisting his words. But Harry knew his father, and he was already reading his thoughts so that he could defend himself.

"Dad, isn't my imagination part of the mind I was given? Aren't there things to understand that can only be known through my spirit and not my eyes?"

John liked it even less when Harry talked about his spirit. What did a boy know about such things?

"Look at all that magic!" said Harry. He took another bite of ice cream. "Wow, it's amazing, Dad! People getting up out of graves, walking on water, frogs falling from the sky, sick people getting well . . . all impossible things but possible because someone believed. Did none of that happen?"

"Of course it did, son."

"And weren't we told to believe? Weren't we told that we would do even more incredible things? Might that be you or might that be me? Weren't we told to become great magicians too? All I am saying, Dad, is—if I, or any of us, have the gift to see what really is—I should be able to do some pretty awesome magic."

His father sighed. "Keep your magic pure, Harry. Don't try and do stuff that's wrong."

Harry thought about how he had attempted to separate Titus Kligore's head from the rest of him. "Okay, you're right, Dad." He understood the wisdom his dad was sharing with him—with great magic comes great responsibility.

They finished their sundaes, and Harry thought, all things considered, it went pretty well for a dad conversation.

John locked the front door and turned out the porch light. Together, he and Harry walked up the stairs to bed. John put his hand on Harry's back. Harry craned his neck slightly forward, afraid that John might attempt to take off his ski cap to tousle his hair.

When Harry reached his bedroom, he dropped his backpack on the floor and ran to the mirror that hung above the chest of drawers. Harry closed his eyes, raised both hands, and pulled the cap from his head.

Breathing deeply—as if to gird himself with strength—he opened his eyes and peered at his reflection.

"Oh wow," he whispered as he stared at the boy in the mirror. What was left of his hair stood upright in patches. His scalp was a wasteland of skin and hair. He thought he looked like Herman Melville Field after Hurricane Delilah hit it last spring.

"I want to destroy that guy," Harry muttered, fuming. He clenched his fists at the mirror and sneered. "I'm going to zing him—wand or no wand. He's the one who won't be showing up tomorrow night." Harry sneered some more as he looked at his pitiful self in the mirror, making himself madder and madder.

"Your magic doesn't work that way," said Rabbit, peeking around from behind Harry. It didn't help that Rabbit was obviously trying to hide a very wide smile behind his furry paws. "You have to let your anger go. The deep magic is not about vengeance."

"Then what is it good for if it doesn't make

me stronger than the bullies?" asked Harry, as he turned angrily from the mirror.

"Come on," said Rabbit. Rabbit opened the door and walked onto the second-floor landing. Firmly planting his ski cap on his head, Harry followed Rabbit down the staircase.

"Hi, Rabbit," said Harvest, as he climbed up the steps. "I love Go-Gurt." He carried five sticks of Go-Gurt in his hands—strawberry, blueberry, and cherry.

97

"Oh, me too," Rabbit said.

"G'night, Rabbit. G'night, Harry," said Harvest.

"He can see you? How is that? I didn't reveal you in a trick," said Harry as they reached the entrance foyer.

"Little kids, musicians, and pregnant women—generally, they see the invisible."

Harry was always learning from Rabbit. As he walked with him, Harry grew calm.

Rabbit, his black-and-white haunches bouncing, walked into the kitchen. "Remember these?" Rabbit pointed to the stenciled words painted along the top of the kitchen wall. "This is what your mother's great-aunt stenciled with love," Rabbit said.

"I know. I have lived here for a while, remember?"

"Then you should know those words by heart, which is the intention. Read them to me,

Harry."

Harry did not want to, but he knew that it would make Rabbit happy. Harry turned around in the kitchen as he read the words out loud: "Love, joy, peace, patience, kindness, goodness, faithfulness, gentleness, and self-control."

Harry looked down at Rabbit. Rabbit's ink-blot face stared back at him.

"Hmmm. I don't see vengeance in that magic, do you, Harry?" asked Rabbit.

"No, Rabbit. I don't."

"However, I do see self-control. Your rabbit and your wand will serve you, Harry. You will have a magical life. It will also be a life full of trouble. We are told that. That is why there will always be times for heroes. Don't be like Titus, Harry. Be the hero you were meant to be. Sleepy Hollow needs you. The world needs you," declared Rabbit.

Harry nodded, looking at the words that

ran beneath the ceiling. "So that's why self-control is up there."

"Exactly," said Rabbit. "You must restrain yourself so that the goodness can emerge. And it takes practice . . . lots of practice. You need to practice that as hard as you do the one arm vanish."

When Harry went to bed that night, he had plenty to think about. He lay awake, staring at the ceiling. In the soft glow of the full moon, his mind caught up with his soul, and he slipped into a deep sleep.

Words have power. Their meaning cuts through time and space, even dimension. As Harry floated on the words of his dreamscape—joy, peace, gentleness—he came to a great white door.

He walked to the door and opened it. Passing through, he was met with three of the largest words he had ever seen. They were brighter than all the shine of New York's Time Square, which Harry had seen last year when his family went to see the Christmas Spectacular at Radio City Music Hall.

The words were tall, taller than Harry without a doubt and maybe taller than Titus. They were not a question. They were a declaration. They spoke to him, etching themselves onto Harry's soul.

"Yes," Harry said. "Yes. I understand. I do!"

Far away, Harry heard the chimes of the grandfather clock in the entranceway. It was midnight. As he awoke from his dream, he heard the clock chimes more clearly. In Sleepy Hollow, midnight signified the tradition of the "witching hour"—the time from midnight to one in the morning when terrible things, by legend, happened. But this was not a witching hour for Harry.

He bolted upright from his sleep as the chimes rang in his ear. He wiped his brow, covered in night sweat. He felt his head. He could not believe it! He jumped from the mattress and rushed over to the mirror above the chest of drawers.

In the half-light of the new day, Harry Moon saw his reflection. How could this be? He touched the top of his head. His hair . . . it had grown back. He took a deep breath and touched it again just in case he was still caught in the dream. But no, this was real. A smile stretched across Harry's face. He was not surprised.

Something had come over him . . . a magic. A magic bigger than himself.

As he turned from the mirror, the shiny letters from his dream stood in the bedroom. They practically blinded him. So that he would not forget them, as he often forgot things in his dreams by the next morning, Harry Moon wrote, with trembling fingers, the words on a sticky note with a Sharpie so he would never, ever, ever forget—the sound, the power, and the beauty of those three words.

DO NO EVIL.

SATURDAY

"Won't you wrinkle your costume, brother dear?" asked Honey as she sat at the breakfast table eating her Cheerios. She was staring at Harry, who was already wearing his red cape for that night's show.

"Polyester doesn't wrinkle," said Harry with an air of authority.

Her brow furrowed, Honey looked closely at Harry. There was writing on his T-shirt, but she just could not make it out beneath the tie of his cape. Harry sat beside Harvest in his booster chair. Harvest was not that hungry, given his late-night snack of five Go-Gurts. Still, Harry played his game of counting Cheerios with his two-year-old brother.

"One," said Harry, as he pushed the first Cheerio across the toddler's placemat. Harvest beamed as he snatched the first Cheerio and pushed it into his mouth.

"One!" echoed Harvest after he had successfully swallowed cereal circle number one. The game continued through number two and number three with Harry prompting, "That's a good boy," after each. Honey found it all too tedious and boring. Honey still could not see more of the lettering beneath Harry's cape. It was hand drawn in black marker on his striped T-shirt.

"Ten!" shouted Harvest as he completed his counting fun with Harry.

"Hey, Superman," Honey said, squinting her eyes, "what's that say underneath your cape?"

"Oh, just a little something I put on so I could remember."

"What do you need to remember?" Honey asked with an air of indifference. "Besides what two plus two equals."

"Ta da!" said Harvest, joining in the fun. He liked it when Harry played magic with him.

Honey got a closer look at Harry's shirt when his cape moved. "Do. No. Evil," Honey said, reading the words slowly as if for effect. "That's just good common sense. Are you saying that is somehow magic?"

"That's just the point, Honey. Magic can be either good or evil." Harry looked around to see if his mother was within earshot. Some things were easier said when parents weren't listening. "We have to always remember to do the good stuff!"

"Do no evil . . . is that your new superhero motto or is that your new name?" asked Honey. "You'll be big stuff after the talent show tonight. You need to be thinking about merchandising. I'm sure Dad would help set up a silkscreen sweatshop in the garage. Maybe you need a manager. A beautiful, smart business manager."

106

"No. Ick. Get away." Harry said. "Do no evil is more for me than for anyone else . . . to remind me of something I should never forget."

Honey was suddenly paying attention. For once, Harry was being real with her, letting her in. Honey did not want to blow her chance with her big brother by giving him any 'tude in her response.

"Whaddaya mean you can't forget?" she asked softly.

"I just can't ever forget where my magic

comes from."

"And where is that?"

"From the Great Magician."

Honey shook her head.

"Are you doing drugs?" she asked. "I hear everyone is doing them in middle school."

"No, I am not! And don't make fun of my magic."

"Yes, don't make fun of his magic," agreed Mary Moon as she walked into the kitchen having just walked their dog, Half Moon. Harvest's face lit up with joy as he saw Rabbit enter the kitchen with his mom and his dog.

"Hey, Rabbit," said Harvest.

"Hey, Harvest," replied Rabbit.

"I want to play with you!"

"We will!" Rabbit said. As he crossed the kitchen, he patted Harvest on the head. "I have to finish something with your brother first." He smiled as he crossed the kitchen and headed into the entranceway.

"That's my Rabbit," said Harvest, proudly.

Mary looked down at her toddler in the booster chair. His mouth was covered in milk and Cheerio mush. She picked up the side of the little one's bib and wiped his mouth clean.

"Harvest, do you have an imaginary friend?"

"No, Mommy," Harvest said. "He's here. You see him?"

Harry tapped his mom's arm. "Generally, Mom, magic rabbits can only be viewed by babies, pregnant ladies, and musicians."

"You mean," asked Mary, "highly intuitive people like musicians or innocents like infants?"

"Hmmm," Harry said, "I never thought of it that way."

"Harrumph," Honey added. She gulped down the rest of her tomato juice. "Apparently, Mother," she continued, "Saint Harry over there has a Holy Lagomorph that only the immature males in the Moon family converse with."

Harvest scrunched up his face in distaste and stuck out his cereal-covered tongue at Honey.

"Sorry, Harvest. But our older brother is driving us mad!"

Harry said nothing. He simply smiled and pointed to the words on his chest.

"Just look at that, Mother!" Honey said pointing at Harry's T-shirt. "Look at what Harry has written on his good shirt. He ruined a good shirt!"

Mary looked over from the sink where she was rinsing the breakfast dishes. "Isn't that nice?" she said. "Do no evil. Nice, Harry. We should send that shirt to Congress."

At that precise moment, Harry's dad walked through the door.

"Look, Daddy," persisted Honey, pointing again to Harry's shirt. "Look what Harry did to his shirt!"

"All right, Harry buddy!" his dad beamed. "Super cool. Kinda like the way we wrapped up the conversation last night?"

"Huh?" Honey said.

"I should remember—I rehearsed it," said John. "'At the very least, keep your magic pure, Harry. Don't try and do stuff that's wrong.'"

111

"Exactly!" said Harry, as he turned his chest to his sister, teasing her with his smile.

"Jumpin' goldfish!" exclaimed Honey. "This family has all gone mad. The next thing I know you will *all* be talking to the rabbit!"

"Don't knock the rabbit," Harry said. "He's flying for the win tonight."

"What does a rabbit have to do with excellence?" asked Honey, fuming.

"Exactly!" said Harry. "You can't be truly excellent without being in step with the good magic. Rabbit helps me with all the words Mom's great-aunt wrote on the kitchen wall."

"All right," said John, as he went over to Harry and tousled his newly-sprouted, full head of hair. "I have an idea, buddy. I like the 'Do No Evil' vibe. You and I could get out the old silk screen and roll out some nice tees. They would be some awesome shirts for my Rotary. Whaddaya say, sport?"

"I say, 'awesome,' Dad!"

"What are you, Harry, a magician or a salesman?" cried Honey. "Make up your mad mind! You are giving me a headache!" Fuming, she jumped up from her chair and stomped her shoes against the kitchen floor.

"I'll get you a drink of water, dear," soothed Mary Moon.

Honey held her head high. She was bloodied but unbowed. Suddenly, she was sprayed with a batch of Cheerios. She looked over at the perpetrator. Harvest Moon, with both of his hands covered in Cheerios, flicked crumbs at her from his booster chair. He incanted his own mojo on Honey.

"A B R A C A D A B R A!" he shouted.

113

114

THE ONE ARM APPEAR

News of the flying rabbit had spread throughout Sleepy Hollow. Everyone wanted to see the bunny fly. So by four o'clock Saturday afternoon, ticket sales ended online. For the first time in its long history, the Scary Talent Show was sold out.

A traditionally popular event, the Scary Talent Show was always packed, but tickets were usually available at the door for last-minute attendees.

Not this night. This was going to be Harry Moon's night. This was the vindication of the little guy, the too-short-to-be-picked scapegoat, and the one who never got the girl. This was the high-minded desire to simply be as good as one could be.

"That's what hard work and discipline can do!" said John Moon, as he rolled the last silk screen T-shirt for Harry in their garage. John was able to get such a good deal at Walgreens on a bulk-buy of plain-colored tees that he printed a shirt for every kid in Harry's homeroom cheering section.

Meanwhile, elsewhere in town, Titus Kligore was not worried. With his bloated sense of self, Titus had convinced himself that Harry Moon would not be there. In fact, he was so sure that he had successfully hazed-out his competition, he convinced his dad, Maximus Kligore, to throw a victory party that night at Chillie Willies.

"Just see to it that you win!" said Mayor Kligore as he slapped his son's back with the great palm of his hand. "I'll get the store manager to order up burgers and fries for the entire eighth grade."

Titus took a deep breath. He wanted more than anything to impress his father—something he hadn't done much. "Sounds like a plan, Dad!" replied Titus. Now maybe his dad would be proud of him. Something had been lost in the father-son relationship between Titus and his father. Winning had become the only thing and at all costs. It was no longer important to play fair and well. Titus enjoyed winning, but sometimes, the cost was just too much.

"After this party tonight," said the mayor, "no one will be able to say that Maximus Kligore doesn't know how to throw a party!"

A hard rain had started to fall, which, of course, was not unusual for Sleepy Hollow. But still, Harry sometimes got tired of the weather in town. He was convinced that Mayor Kligore had something to do with it. It always seemed like autumn in Sleepy Hollow.

Ring. Ring. It was the landline at the Moon household on Nightingale Lane.

"Hello?" said Harry.

"It's goodbye for you, hairy moon-butt," said the rough, low voice. "Don't even think about coming tonight."

The caller tried to disguise his voice, but Harry recognized it. He had heard it in the dark. It was a voice meant to scare him by showing its power and depth. It was Titus.

Before Harry could hang up the phone, Titus hung up first. Both of them were pretty

good at hanging up. They had lots of practice.

This was about the tenth time that Titus had threatened Harry that day. It was almost time to leave, and Harry was becoming worried. What if he was waiting for him again? What if he planned something worse than a haircut? But there was no time for worry. Harry had a show to perform.

He texted Sarah Sinclair to see if she could come early.

"Yes," she texted back.

An hour later, Harry, Rabbit, and Sarah sat quietly on the couch in the family room of the Moon house. The sun was already setting, the last of it slanting through the blinds. Harry closed the door.

"Uh oh. This looks serious," commented Sarah.

120

"It is," Harry replied, walking over to the sofa. He took a seat between Rabbit and his ex-babysitter.

Harry could not help but notice how really nice Sarah looked in her Scheherazade veils, bangles, and hooped earrings. Still, Sarah's natural beauty could not quell Harry's anxious heart. Nervously, he tapped Wand on the coffee table, as if to dislodge the answer of what to do.

"What's wrong?" Sarah asked. "I see fear and courage in your eyes. 'Courage, after all, is not the lack of fear. Courage is pressing forward in spite of the fear.' I think C.S. Lewis said something like that."

"Keep this on the down low," Harry said softly. "Titus Kligore has been threatening me all afternoon, making calls like a slasher right out of Scream Four."

"Wow!" said Sarah. "He is really taking this Maniacs thing seriously."

"What's the solution?" asked Harry.

121

"You're holding it in your hand," replied Rabbit. Harry looked down at the wand.

"But I tried that," Harry said. "It didn't work. The wand didn't work."

"Harry," Rabbit said, "that is because you tried to use it for vengeance. Your magic has a heart, a good heart, and can only be used for good. Like when you made the chestnut tree bloom. Your heart was light then."

"And the next time I used it, I tried to hide

Titus's head . . . remember? Nothing happened."

"And you know why."

"Because I was angry. Deep down in my heart and soul, I was angry and wanted to get back at Titus for what he did."

"That's just the point," explained Rabbit. "This magic does not work from anger."

"But, I'm not angry, now. I'm scared."

"Then use your magic to hide yourself from your enemy. As you grow, your magic will grow, and you will come to a deep understanding of just how powerful it is when you use it for good."

"It can do that?"

"It can do anything that is good."

"Wow!" said Harry. "I love you, Rabbit! Where did you come from, anyway?"

Rabbit looked at Sarah.

"Well," Sarah shuffled her feet underneath the coffee table, looking at Rabbit. "He was free. I didn't want to tell you, Harry. I thought you might think less of me or of Rabbit. I tried to pay for Rabbit at the Sleepy Hollow Magic Shoppe, but that nice old man at the store refused. He said since Rabbit was the deep magic, he couldn't charge."

"Are you serious?" said Harry.

123

"I am priceless. Am I not?" Rabbit asked.

Even though Harry always enjoyed a good debate with Rabbit, he did not respond. He was too filled with performance anxiety. The show was only an hour away.

"Calm down, Harry," Rabbit said. "You know your material, and we can practice the one arm vanish on the way."

Sarah stood up from the sofa, her bangles and hoops clanging against her skin. "I am so excited!" she cried. Harry looked at her and thought how absolutely beautiful she was.

Sarah was sixteen. Her father had given her the keys to the family's blue Ford pickup so she could take Harry to the show. Each of the twelve contestants had to get to the auditorium an hour early for roll call and last-minute costume and makeup changes. Harry's family was going to be leaving later for the school auditorium.

Harry rode shotgun. Rabbit sat in the backseat. Sarah drove like a pro. In an attempt to not feel tiny or small, Harry sat up tall in his seat, acting casual, for he had never seen his ex-babysitter drive. "Really nice on the turns, Sarah."

"Thank you, Harry," Sarah said. "I do have one other thing to say."

"What's that?" Harry asked.

"While he wouldn't take the money for Rabbit, Mr. Dupree did ask if he could come to the show tonight. He said he thought you should be encouraged."

"Samson Dupree, really?" Harry asked. "He wants to come to my show?"

"He knows more than you think he knows," Sarah said, raising her eyebrows. "I'll say only one thing more and then I will stay silent on the matter. I think Samson Dupree is your guardian angel!"

"My guardian angel?" said Harry. His eyes went glassy.

"Yes," said Sarah. "He watches over you."

"I don't even know what that means—a guardian angel. Are there such things?"

"I think there are. At least, now I do. It seems like you are his guy."

"I thought I was Rabbit's guy."

"I am from the deep magic, goof. I'm not an

angel," added Rabbit from the backseat.

"Stop!" said Harry. "I see him!"

"See who?" Sarah asked, looking over the wheel at the horizon.

"Titus Kligore. He and the other goons are at the curb in the parking lot, waiting for us!" Harry said nervously. "Stop the truck! I have to get into one arm vanish mode!"

Without a prompt, as if he knew all along what he must do, Harry raised his arm up in front of him, his red cape falling in front of his eyes—an invisible curtain now hid their bodies.

Together, entangled in the fabric of the cosmos, Harry, Sarah, and Rabbit intoned in unison,
"A B R A C A D A B R A!"

With a wave of his wand, Harry vanished under the invisibility of his cape.

While the pickup truck was still stopped in the middle of the street, the passenger door opened and closed all by itself, or so it appeared to the outside world. No one could see the now invisible Harry Moon.

"Hey!" said Titus Kligore, looking across the school parking lot in his convincing Freddie costume. "Isn't that Harry Moon's ex-babysitter in that Ford truck?"

"Where?" asked Finn, with a large hockey mask over his face, as he was dressed in his Jason outfit.

"There!" said Titus.

Titus and the Maniacs looked across the parking lot, filling up with incoming cars. There was no Ford truck. Titus blinked and shook his head. "I must be getting paranoid. I could've sworn that was Harry Moon in a truck with Sarah Sinclair. Watch, guys—that Harry Moon is a sneaky one."

The invisible Harry was now riding on top

of the pickup cab as the truck turned into the parking lot, hidden from view under the folds of his invisible cape. Neither passersby nor Titus could see the moving truck under the veil of Harry's magic cape.

"Can you see where to drive?" Harry called out to Sarah. The cape covered everything on the truck, including the windshield.

"Just fine," said Sarah. She drove as slowly as the lead car in a small-town Fourth of July parade. "This was *not* part of drivers' ed, that's for sure!" she added, laughing.

Unseen, Sarah navigated the Ford pickup cautiously through the parking lot, arriving at the curb of the sidewalk that led to the front doors of the school.

With his right hand fully extended, the cape fell from his arm. Harry slipped down the body of the truck. Crouching behind the cape so he would not be spotted, Harry walked to the driver's door and opened it. Sarah scooted from the seat and stepped onto the ground. She hunched down behind the cape, hidden from Titus and the Maniacs' view.

"Come on," Harry said to Rabbit.

Rabbit laughed. "Don't worry about me. I'll meet you backstage. You got this."

"Okay," said Harry in a whisper. "Sarah, just follow my steps."

"Will do," she replied. Together, behind the cape, Harry and Sarah walked toward the school building. In front of them, waiting under the weather awning, were Titus and his Maniacs, scanning the crowd for any trace of Harry.

Together, but hidden and frightened, Sarah and Harry proceeded carefully on their walk of invisibility to the school doors. The invisible cloth of the cape could not touch the ground — otherwise, one of the two or both of them might trip on it and fall. There was just the slightest view of their feet as they walked.

Harry looked in front of him at the school entrance. He kept his focus on his destination, not on the fear he felt about the bully and his gang.

"Look," Titus said. "Do you see what I see?"

"What?" asked Finn.

"Look over there! Feet walking—nothing but feet walking! What the heck!" Titus shouted, pointing at the sidewalk.

As the Maniacs looked down at the sidewalk, there was nothing. Harry and Sarah had already walked past them.

"I don't see nothin'," said Finn.

Titus was unconvinced. He was sure that he had seen feet. He looked out at the parking lot, and he saw what he thought he had seen before.

"I'm not going crazy, guys," he said. "I just saw feet, and I know I saw Sarah Sinclair's truck before 'cuz there it is!" He pointed again and, this time, at the end of his finger was Sarah Sinclair's blue truck parked at the curb. He ran to it, and the Maniacs ran too, not knowing what else to do.

"I knew it! I knew it!" Titus shouted, clutching the handle on the door of the truck. "Those sneaky ones are here!"

"What do you mean, they are here?" asked the guy dressed as the Werewolf. "How could they have gotten here?"

131

"Magic," Titus said. "Real magic."

"Wicked magic?" asked Finn.

"I don't know. I can't be sure," said Titus, as he turned away from the truck door.

Even though all the Maniacs were in masks or clay makeup, their eyes betrayed the fear that was in their hearts. They were wondering— who was this Harry Moon character and what type of magic was he playing with?

"Come on, guys, we are letting our competitors get the best of us," said Titus. "There is no such thing as real magic. It's all tables and chairs. Now, let's go win this dang thing."

Meanwhile, Harry, Sarah, and Rabbit were already backstage, getting ready for the performance that would change their lives forever.

THE SCARY TALENT SHOW

"Miss Pryor, I don't mean to be a snitch," Titus said with more than a twinge of haughtiness, "but I do *not* believe that Harry Moon is competing in good sportsmanship." He towered over the drama and arts teacher, cornering her in the hallway.

"Why do you say that?" Miss Pryor sighed. She knew Titus's tactics too well. The Kligore family was accustomed to getting its way at any cost.

"I think that Sarah Sinclair is doing more than assisting. That's against the rules," complained Titus.

"I have seen nothing in their show that would justify your accusation," Miss Pryor said with a huff.

"And what about that stupid rabbit? That's no rabbit. He's a beast. Did you see the size of that thing? Some kind of monster. You better keep an eye on it," he said. "You wait for it, Miss Pryor. It's the rabbit that's running the show." Titus spoke so fast he had to stop and catch a breath. "It's not even Harry doing it—it's some kind of black magic. My father, the mayor, supports the idea of Spooky Town, but not that kind of magic—not black magic!"

"Thank you, Titus. I am sure our judges will be watching carefully."

Miss Pryor pushed some stray hairs behind her ears. With her clipboard at her side, she walked backstage to the stage manager. "Has Harry Moon signed in?" she asked.

"I think so," the stage manager said. He flipped through some pages on his clipboard. "Yep." He pointed to Harry's signature. "Signed in at six twenty. But I haven't seen him since."

135

Miss Pryor played by the rules. She did not particularly like Titus Kligore's oppressive personality, but something that Titus had said was rattling her.

The show began promptly at seven o'clock. Miss Pryor stepped into the yellowish spotlight on the stage and announced the eighth Annual Scary Talent Show. Miss Pryor was high energy. Her smile gleamed into the packed audience. There were even people sitting on the aisle steps in the balcony. Miss Pryor began the evening by congratulating the many "wonderful" acts from "many of our talented students."

The Maniacs were on board first. The Maniacs came out on stage and began to sing in front of the curtain. It all seemed rather average.

Titus had a strong baritone voice. Despite his unfair tactics, Titus was a terrific singer. The Maniacs sang the hit song, "Let's Get Hysterical," with astounding a cappella skill. The curtains parted to reveal a stark, wintry landscape.

As the Maniacs' song continued, their costumes were transformed before the audience's eyes. At the crescendo of the song, the singing group morphed into snarling wolves. The technical brilliance of the act could not be denied. As the Maniacs hunched down on the floor, a massive orb fell from the rafters, suspended in the air like a full moon. Black crows from the skeleton trees took flight, cutting silhouettes across the moon while the Maniacs all howled. The audience went wild with applause and whistles.

Harry, Rabbit, and Sarah watched from stage left. Harry studied the Maniacs' act. "They added the crows since dress rehearsal," he said.

Sarah nodded. "Yeah. I guess it helps when your dad owns the biggest costume and special effects store in Sleepy Hollow."

"He has a bunch of money to do fancy stuff like that," said Harry. He pulled the backstage curtain enough to be able to look out at the audience. He was surprised. They gave the Maniacs thunderous applause but no standing ovation.

"We gotta play fair," said Sarah.

"I know," said Harry, turning away from the curtain. He looked up at his ex-babysitter. She was so beautiful. He sighed. "Thank you, Sarah, for helping me out."

"No problemo," Sarah said, smiling.

"I hope someday you will see me not as a guy you used to babysit, but just as a guy."

"I do, Harry. I already do. I wouldn't be here if I didn't care about you. But you know, Harry, there will always be the age difference between us."

Harry was beside himself. *Wow! Listen to her. She already sees me as a guy! I am making progress, and she hasn't even gotten my Christmas present.* Harry returned the smile. He wanted to say more, so much more, but all he could muster was, "That's a nice crown you are wearing."

"Oh, thanks! Do you like it? I added it at the last minute. It's actually called a 'diadem,' and it has a little veil. I got the idea from an old television show called *I Dream of Jeannie.*"

While the other acts took the stage and performed, Titus lurked backstage, hunting down Harry and Sarah. There were no clues. No one had seen them. Of course, Harry and Sarah were wrapped in the magic of the cape of invisibility.

Harry Moon's heart knocked against his ribcage as Miss Pryor walked onto the stage to introduce the final act. Harry looked out at the judges' table next to the orchestra pit. The three judges were engaged, still fresh. *Being last can cut both ways,* Harry thought.

As Harry took the invisible cloak away, revealing both himself and Sarah, the stage manager came up to them. "There you guys are!" the manager said. "I gotta get your mics on." With rapid-fire efficiency, he clipped the wireless mics on both Harry and Sarah.

"Ladies and gentlemen! We are pleased to present Sleepy Hollow's final act of the evening—The Amazing Magic Show of Harry Moon—starring eighth-grader Harry Moon, assisted by Sarah Sinclair."

Harry put on his thrift store top hat. He turned to Sarah, who adjusted it on his head.

"Go get 'em, Moon Man," she said, smiling.

Harry looked into her soft, blue eyes. He thought he would fall in. *I believe in you*, they blinked back.

This was it! She's going to kiss me on my

lips. Alas, not yet—but a thoughtful kiss on the cheek was more than enough for the moment.

Harry smiled at Sarah and, with a wink, took a deep breath and turned to meet his audience.

To a sparse splattering of applause, Harry marched onto center stage. He looked like a cartoon character. His black, velvet top hat was too big for his short, spark plug body. Beneath the single spotlight, he stood—a lonesome, solitary figure—quite the contrast to Titus's loud and boisterous group.

141

"Good evening, ladies and gentlemen," Harry said. He stood quietly, waiting for the silence to collect itself. Then he stood there even longer. Someone coughed in the auditorium, and the sound thundered in the hush.

In the thirty-fifth row on the first level of the auditorium, Mary Moon grabbed her husband's hand.

"Harry has stage fright! He's not saying anything." Mary whispered through clenched teeth.

"Come on, sport," said John, encouraging his son. Harry looked out at the packed crowd. His eyes swept the audience. He saw his family. He saw Samson Dupree. Then he saw the entire Kligore family, including the mayor, Maximus Kligore. Seated in the row behind them were several of Kligore's We Drive By Night staff. John swallowed and whispered to Mary, "Mayor Kligore and his . . . company are here."

Honey looked at her brother standing like a statue on the stage. She felt the blood drain from her face. "I knew this would happen," she proclaimed to her parents. "He's choking up out there! I won't live this down. I am ruined. Harry Moon, you are a menace."

Harvest sat in Honey's lap and reached up with his tiny hand and put his gooey fingers into her mouth. He wasn't playing with her tongue—he was silencing it.

But Harry wasn't choking. He was seizing his moment, making sure that the audience was completely with him. All eyes—including the eyes of one Titus Kligore—were focused on the stage, waiting, hushed, riveted in the silence, to see what this young magic man would do. "I just knew it," Titus said, seething to Finn and Freddie. "Check it out, boys. I told you he was a sneaky one. Look it! He even got himself a wig."

143

Harry straightened up to his full, straight height. He beamed a smile. And in the instant of that radiant smile, the audience became Harry's personal plaything. *Everything was going to be all right.* The crowd let out a collective sigh, assured that this funny-looking performer with the top hat knew exactly what he was doing. Harry was running the show from his small circle of spotlight. Harry Moon had learned well by studying the master illusionist, Elvis Gold.

"It's strange being here, don't you think?"

he asked the crowd as he walked across the stage. "The mystery never leaves us."

Mary Moon shuddered, "Oh no." Her grasp on her husband's hand went tighter. "What is he doing?"

"I'm not quite sure, sweetheart," said John, the effervescent encourager of his son.

"I'm not speaking of this stage," said Harry, addressing the audience. "I am speaking of the wonderful mystery of life."

"It's strange, being visitors in this world. As hard as we try, we don't quite get it. We see glimpses of something more. A deeper magic. I see it in my little brother's eyes. I see it in the beauty of the sunrise."

Harry extended his arms wide open to the audience. "But, as hard as any of us try, we don't ever have all the answers. So tonight, please sit back and relax, as I hope to take you through a doorway into the wonder that lies behind that sunrise. Sarah Sinclair, if you will assist me?"

With her genie scarves trailing behind, Sarah walked onto the stage. Her smile was as bright as the spotlight. Sarah had no idea what was about to happen, but she didn't care.

Sarah was a very graceful assistant. She was a junior in high school, after all. She was liked by most of the girls in middle school. They looked up to her, and she had a good eye for fashion too. Her fan club liked her outfit, especially her diadem with the veil.

Harry had silenced everyone. The auditorium was hushed. This was the show they had come for.

Sarah smiled reassuringly as she reached Harry. Harry tipped his hat knowingly to her and took her hand to introduce her to the audience. Sarah curtsied like they were royalty. He was the king. She was the queen. His tipping of the hat and her curtsy were lovely signs of respect toward one another. The audience clapped in appreciation.

"How adorable," Mary said.

"If you like kitties with bows and unicorns," Honey said. She folded her arms across her chest with a "Harummph."

"What does *that* mean?" asked John.

"Cheese ball," answered Honey scrunching herself down into her seat. "I told him he needed new tricks."

Harry handed his top hat to Sarah. She held it, walking to the rim of the stage, revealing the emptiness inside of the hat to the audience members and to the judges.

When Sarah returned to him, Harry opened his palm.

"A B R A C A D A B R A," he commanded.

Harry turned his palm in the sleight of hand. He turned it back to the audience and there, in the grasp of his fingers, was the almond-wood wand! With Sarah at his side,

Harry placed the wand above and below the hat, running it through the empty spaces to show the audience there were no wires or a hidden cabinet supporting the hat.

With a grand gesture, Harry waved the wand over the hat, saying, "A B R A C A D A B R A!"

Mayor Maximus Kligore looked on from the third row behind the orchestra pit. Watching carefully, he squinted. He had even brought his bird-watching binoculars along, just in case Harry Moon made it to the stage. He was studying the magician's every move. He would expose the fraud and save the trophy for the Kligores. Titus must win.

147

"That's odd," muttered Maximus to his assistant, Cherry Tomato, from behind the binoculars. "That wand Harry Moon is using is not made of yew wood."

"How can you tell that from here?" Cherry asked. She had the most unusual eyes— cat-like. "What is it? A popsicle stick?"

"No. No. You fool. I have never seen one before. It's made from almond wood."

"So?"

"Almond wood. That's the same wood, so the story goes, that was used in Moses's staff for all those miracles."

Cherry Tomato sat up with a bolt as if she had just been given a shot with a very long needle. She grimaced—a look that suggested she did not like what her boss said. No, not one bit.

Meanwhile, on stage, Harry reached his hand into the top hat. The audience drew in its collective breath. They had heard stories about this young one. No one knew what to expect.

Harry's arm fumbled around inside the hat, stretching, until he hit on something. His body stiffened. As he yanked, the hat yanked back. The smile on Harry's face froze. His arm disappeared down into the hat. Harry

148

was lifted into the air like a kite by the pull of the magic. With Sarah struggling to hold the top hat firm, Harry's head, shoulders, and chest disappeared into the top hat.

Slish slash, went his legs, wig-wagging back and forth in the air, upside down out of the hat. The crowd gasped. In the middle of the spotlight stood Sarah—all alone—her face straining, gallantly fighting to hold the wiggling hat upright, half of Harry inside it, his legs swimming in space. No one could be that strong to hold that hat upright for very long.

149

The audience rose to its feet in a mixture of fear and awe. Some people screamed.

Sarah turned the hat over to the side, holding it firmly between her arms. Harry's scissoring legs flipped sideways with the hat. She turned the hat toward the audience, with the real, live kicking boy inside.

Sarah then flipped the hat over, and Harry's feet hit the floor. As they did, he let out a big "Ah ha!"

His feet—and only his feet—were on solid ground.

Never had there been anything like this before in the Sleepy Hollow Middle School. Harry was running around the stage like a cartoon with just his legs and feet sticking out of the hat. There was no sign of the rest of him. It was both scary and comical.

"Ladies and gentlemen! May I introduce Sleepy Hollow's very own Headless Magician!" proclaimed Sarah.

The audience did not know whether to applaud or call the fire department. They were on their feet, screaming. The hat stopped running—the spotlight flying to it.

The hat took a bow.

Transfixed, the audience watched as Harry's legs buckled to the floor and his body wrestled inside the hat.

Mimicking the sounds of the thousands of hours of cartoons he had watched as a kid, Harry created a pandemonium of fighting noises inside the top hat. With the speaker system at full tilt, the theater reverberated with the imagination of his soul.

"Cartoons!" yelled Harvest, jumping up and down on his sister's lap. "Cartoons! Harry *knows* I like 'em best!"

151

"Big deal," replied Honey.

As Harry wrestled on the floor, he leveraged himself with the hat, attempting with great determination to free himself. First, his chest popped out and then his shoulders. Finally, his head and his arms appeared.

The spotlight burned hot as Harry lay exhausted and sweaty on the floor, fully revealed except for his hands. Rolling his back against the floorboards, Harry struggled upward until he was standing upright, his hands still inside the hat.

With her scarves flowing, Sarah approached the hat. With the precision of a registered nurse, she began to pull on it from the other side. As she did, Harry's hands were exposed, holding what looked like a huge white snowball. But as Sarah pulled further, it was not a snowball at all. It was white fur . . . and then more white fur . . . and then black fur . . . and then gray and black-and-white fur. There, like a banner unfurling, was the largest, lop-eared Harlequin rabbit anyone had ever seen!

In the audience, Samson Dupree, his hair

pomaded flat so that people behind him could see, sat back and smiled like a proud papa. He leaned over to a set of five-year-old twins and said, "Wow! That was some hat trick, don't you think?"

"Epic!" said the twins in unison.

Samson turned to the twins' father and handed him his Sleepy Hollow Magic Shoppe card. "Come by the store sometime if you want a rabbit all your own. I don't take cash or credit cards. The rabbits are free."

153

"Oh, I don't know," said the father.

"No rabbit pen necessary. No upkeep. You just gotta show love and respect to a little rabbit. "

"Yes!" cried the twins, in unison. Yet it was not in response to anything Samson Dupree said. It was what they were watching on the stage.

Rabbit stood quietly before the audience. His black-and-white face, like a clown mask shining from beneath the spotlight, smiled as he took a bow.

"What?" Harry said as if Rabbit were talking. "You don't want to go back into the hat?"

Rabbit shook his head, "No."

"Then where will you go?" asked Sarah, listening as if the rabbit was talking.

"You want to go flying?" asked Harry.

Rabbit nodded his head, "Yes!"

The audience was silent. This is what they had heard about. They had come to see the rabbit fly. They did not want to miss anything—not one bit.

"Are you going to fly like the wind?" Sarah asked.

Rabbit nodded. His long ears brushed the stage floor.

"You want to blow wherever you please so we will hear your sound, but we won't know from where you come or where you are going?" Harry asked.

Rabbit nodded excitedly.

Harry walked over to Rabbit. He picked up his top hat and put it back on his head. There was even a bit of a swagger in Harry's saunter.

"Then you know what we have to say about that, Sarah?"

"Oh, I do," she replied with a smile.

"It's really quite simple . . . a simple word—abracadabra. Can the audience say it with us?" Harry said, raising his voice.

"Yes! Yes!" the audience thundered. Even Titus couldn't help himself and hollered, "YES!"

"Good," Harry replied. "Then, on the

count of three. One. Two. Three!"

"A B R A C A D A B R A!" the audience yelled.

"I CAN'T HEAR YOU!" Harry shouted back.

"A B R A C A D A B R A!" the audience repeated.

"What is this, a rock concert?" asked Honey. Harvest laughed, putting his fingers in Honey's mouth again.

The people in the audience lifted their eyes as Rabbit rose silently from the stage. Like an untethered helium balloon, Rabbit floated gently, effortlessly. Once he reached the top of the proscenium, he turned his face to the audience.

He sailed—not swam—across the ceiling. This time he did not paddle with his haunches or paws.

The houselights were turned down low for

156

the show on stage. There was no need to turn them up now for everyone could see the sailing rabbit because he seemed to carry his own light. They watched Rabbit, but everyone would tell you later they were watching something other than a rabbit. They were a witness to the deep magic.

Rabbit's fur expanded as he sailed, growing into a great, silver cloud. At the top of his flight—as Rabbit fell from the ceiling above the audience—he broke apart into snowy particles. The auditorium was filled with the gentle flurry.

157

As Rabbit fell like snow flurries, the audience's eyes were redirected by the spinning trajectory of the snowflakes back toward the stage. It was snowing everywhere, even on stage upon Harry and Sarah. It was silent. Like the first snow on warm soil, it did not stick. The silver snowflakes simply vanished into thin air.

"Thank you, everyone!" said Harry. "May the magic never leave you!"

Sarah came up behind him. She unclasped his cape and dropped it from his shoulders. And there it was.

"Hey, those letters turned out well, don't you think?" said John Moon to Mary.

"They look great, John," Mary replied, still a bit dazed.

On the stage, Harry was wearing one of the tees that he and his dad had silk-screened that afternoon.

DO NO EVIL

What happened next that night is still spoken about today in Sleepy Hollow. When Sarah dropped the cape from Harry's shoulders, the amazed audience stood in silence, taking in the young magician, his assistant, and the magic that had filled the auditorium.

Someone from the third row (they say

it was one of Titus's gang) was the first. With a shout of "Bravo!" he started to clap furiously. The theater was filled with shouts of appreciation and thunderous applause, which seemed to go on forever.

Harry had given them the show they had come for.

"Do no evil" was what they wanted to do, after all. Even though it was sometimes hard, people wanted to do good. As Harry Moon said, "There is deep magic in all of us."

159

160

Loss

Titus and his Maniacs won the Scary Talent Show. Before she revealed the winner, Miss Pryor announced that The

Amazing Magic Show of Harry Moon act had been disqualified. She was expecting the moans and groans and shouts of "FIXED!" from the audience, and she got them.

"The judges have ruled that under Rule Four, Section G, the performance is disqualified because of a co-performer who was not on the middle school roster," she explained.

"Sarah Sinclair only assisted," shouted John Moon, standing at his seat.

"It is not because of Sarah Sinclair, John," said Miss Pryor. "It was because of the . . . er . . . the exceptional rabbit. The judges believed that the rabbit was not, for lack of a better expression, a prop, but rather the rabbit co-performed with Harry Moon, executing stunts that would be reserved for a performer, not a prop. And Rabbit is not registered in middle school."

When Titus and the Maniacs were declared the winners, there were a lot of haters, including almost everyone in the eighth grade. The biggest haters of all were Harry Moon's friends—Hao, Bailey, and Declan.

"I'm gonna punch that guy at his own party!" said Bailey. "Who's with me?" Bailey was always ready for a fight.

Declan and Hao said they were with him, but they suggested they just scare Titus instead. They knew Chillie Willies fairly well. They would entrap Titus Kligore inside the Haunted Cube and run frightening clips from the top one hundred scariest movies of all time and drive him mad.

"Hey, guys, I appreciate your sentiments, but just let it go, okay?" said Harry.

"We'll see," said Bailey, which was code for "no."

They were standing outside on the covered sidewalk of the middle school. The parking lot was humming with the departing crowd.

"Great show! Fantastic, Harry! Bummer on the ruling. You should have won!" came the shouts to Harry from everywhere. Many simply came up and interrupted the guys in order to pat Harry on the back or to shake his hand.

These interruptions were fine for Declan, Bailey, and Hao. It was easier to bear their discomfort with Harry's attractive ex-babysitter standing right next to them.

"Are you going to the weasel's party?" Declan asked Harry.

"I think I should show, don't you?" Harry shoved his hands in his pockets. "Good sportsmanship and all that."

"I think that's the right thing to do," Sarah said.

"Good sportsmanship?" Bailey asked. "From whom? Not that scum of a bully! 'Fire with fire' I say!"

"It just shows who is the bigger man," said Harry. "That's all."

"Bigger man?" said Declan. "You lost, buddy. That's how it will read Monday in the school paper."

"I won! I had the good magic," Harry replied.

"Really? Where's your trophy? Oh? You don't have it? That's because you were robbed of it!"

The selectman from the judges' table came up to the group. "Your show was spectacular, young man," he said, as he reached out and shook Harry's hand. "I'm sorry that the rules could not allow for the appropriate public acknowledgment."

"Thank you, sir," Harry said with a smile.

The selectman backed away from the others and walked to a black town car. The other judges waited for him. They were happy and talkative, pouring themselves into the car.

"Look at them," said Hao. "A bunch of sad hypocrites. Look at that! What the heck is that on the bumper? We Drive By Night? The fix was in. You never had a chance, Harry. Mayor Kligore made sure you didn't win. That stinks."

Harry winced at the sight of the We Drive By Night bumper sticker that was also on the bumper of the car that almost ran him down when he visited Samson Dupree at the Sleepy Hollow Magic Shoppe.

"I am telling you all right now . . . this town is not what it seems," said Bailey. "It is not some quaint little Spooky Town, selling quaint spooky trinkets and Headless Horseman dolls to tourists. This town is the real deal. It is evil to its core. One minute, the town is in bankruptcy. The next minute, the selectmen who run the town with the mayor are driving around in limousines!"

Harry agreed. "I know." He watched the limo disappear down the road. He'd always known.

"So, are you coming with us, Harry?"

"I can drive you, if you would like," Sarah told Harry. "The truck is right over there."

"You have a truck?" said Hao, impressed and trying not to show it.

"It's my dad's."

"Hey, thanks, Sarah," Harry said, "but I need a few minutes to myself."

Hao, Bailey, and Declan started to walk away to the party. They were so not able to understand girls.

"You coming, Harry?" said Bailey, turning around.

"Ah . . . Er . . .," Harry said, confused, turning

to Sarah. "I gotta figure out what . . ."

"Oh," said Bailey, "We get it. You gotta figure out about the truck."

"Something like that," said Harry.

Once the guys were gone, and most of the cars had left, Harry sat down on the stone bench on the covered sidewalk and let his disappointment come through. Tears welled in his eyes. He swiped them away, but still, a few tears escaped and ran down his cheeks. It had been an exciting but difficult night.

"I'm sorry," he said, as Sarah sat down beside him. He tried to hide his face with his arm. But he was tired and not really wanting to do a one arm vanish. "I didn't want you to see me like this."

Sarah slipped the purple veil off her costume, bunched it up, and handed it to Harry for a much-needed handkerchief. "That's okay. I've seen tears before," Sarah said. "After all, I was your babysitter."

"Oh, yeah. Right!" Harry said, remembering, as he blew his nose into the purple veil. He looked up at her with his wet eyes. "But you don't see me that way anymore, right?"

"Right," she answered.

"So maybe time will change things, right?" he asked.

"Time will change all of us. But I will always be a girl who is three years older than the boy. Think of it! When you are a freshman next year, I'll be a senior. I'm afraid that this just cannot be."

"Don't say that, Sarah! I don't like it when you talk that way."

"This girl has always talked that way, Harry —ever since I stopped babysitting you. I have never misled you. Have I, Harry?"

"I guess not," he answered as he blew into the veil again.

Rabbit appeared and sat between the two of them on the bench. He put one paw around Harry and his other paw around Sarah.

"I simply want to get this on record," Rabbit said gently, but with enthusiasm.

"As far as love is concerned, both of you need to promise me—because many, many people will try to separate me from you—promise me that you won't ever leave me."

"If you promise us that you will never desert us," Harry replied.

"Never, ever, ever!" said Rabbit.

"Then it's a deal," Harry said.

"Deal?" Rabbit asked Sarah.

"Deal," she replied.

"I'm sorry about tonight," Rabbit said. "But the world is not fair. That's why it needs heroes. It probably won't get any easier."

Harry nodded. He knew Rabbit spoke truth.

"Sarah. Harry," Rabbit continued. "I am going to break it to you gently—having a friend like me has its consequences."

THE HAUNTED CUBE

By the time Sarah and Harry pulled up in the Ford pickup, Chillie Willies was jumping. Neon signs flashed Congratulations, Maniacs! The winning, gold trophy was in the center of the main showroom. Titus Kligore and his Maniacs stood by the trophy for the photo ops. Within minutes, Instagram was flooded with Maniacs shots. It looked like the entire eighth grade— about two hundred in total—had shown up for the party.

Meanwhile, Declan and Bailey had a reputation with their classmates for being trustworthy. By telling Harry's story, they were able to stir up a deep sense of injustice in the hearts of their friends. Most of them had also experienced being bullied by Titus. It was easy to stir up the hate. There were at least three dozen girls and boys working together to scare Titus out of his senses. "Not that he has much sense to begin with," said Hao.

In fact, they had so many students in on the gag, they had already rigged Chillie Willies's Haunted Cube to enact vengeance against Titus.

The Cube was a hot ticket in the showroom. It involved a test of not only courage but of will. It was a virtual haunted house walled with forty LED screens that showed all manner of scary stuff—like floating eyeballs, worms, brains, and skeletons. You were essentially locked in

174

the cube until you screamed. Then, you were taken out of it.

Adele Cracken held the record for the longest time in the cube. She survived for a whopping three minutes and twelve seconds.

The PTA had been trying to shut down the Haunted Cube for years, calling it a nightmare provoker, but Maximus Kligore always won out with his "good, clean, scary fun" pitch.

That night, Clooney Mackay, a super-brilliant techie, split the data that ran into each existing screen into four quadrants. According to Clooney, there would not just be forty scary movies playing at once but 160 of them.

"Heck," Clooney had said, his eyes bouncing with electric excitement, "even the peaceful Dalai Lama would go bonkers inside the Cube."

"This won't kill Titus, will it?" asked Bailey. "I promised Harry we would just mess him up."

"Of course it won't kill him," Clooney said, laughing in anticipation. "But this will be a Halloween he will never forget!"

While kids danced and munched on party snacks, something else was going on at the party. Everyone was texting their own nasty photos and videos of Titus to Clooney's cell phone. The cell fed into his computer. "All the nastiness is from him," said Clooney to his girlfriend, PJ McDonald. "It's about time he got a whiff of his stinky self."

"This is pure evil," complained PJ as she parked both hands on her hips and huffed. She was standing by Clooney's laptop at the back of the Haunted Cube while several of their classmates rigged the guts of the LED screens with the feed cable.

"It is not evil, PJ! An eye for an eye, right?" Clooney said.

"You obviously did not read far enough in the book," PJ replied. "It's 'turn the other cheek.'"

"Fine. We'll turn his cheek once he gives us an eye!"

"Jerks! All of you!" PJ said, looking at her friends in exasperation. As she walked away from Clooney, she tossed her curly, brown hair to accentuate her disapproval.

Several of the students spoke to Maximus Kligore in the party favor section of the store.

"Where did Titus get that singing voice, Mr. Kligore? It is so awesome! It must have come from you."

"Well, I did sing in the choir until my voice changed," Maximus said with pride.

Meanwhile, in the costume showroom, Larry "the Locksmith" Loneghan was busy behind the door of the Haunted Cube. Since his dad ran the Loneghan Hardware Store, Larry spent a lot of growing-up time making extra keys for customers. Larry became an expert on locks. He found a way to override the safety system in the Cube.

"As Mayor Kligore would say, this is just 'good, clean, scary fun,' right?" Larry said to Hao, who was looking over his rigging.

"That's one way of putting it, Larry," said Hao.

So many people were busy scheming that no one noticed Harry, in his cape, and Sarah, in her genie silks, walking through the front door of Chillie Willies.

"Are you sure you are okay with this?" asked Harry, looking up at the beautiful Sarah. He practically had to shout over the loud music.

"Why wouldn't I be?" shouted Sarah.

"It's eighth grade." He shrugged his caped shoulders.

"So?" she said with a smile. "It's nothing to be embarrassed about. We all go through eighth grade at some point."

"Let's hit the snack table," Harry suggested.

"I'm with that." Sarah followed Harry through the crowd. The music was loud, the dancing was fast—but Harry knew something else was at work. Harry sensed it in his soul. His intuition kicked in. There was tension in the air. As if they were waiting for something to happen, no one was talking.

"What would you like?" Sarah asked as she arrived at the snack table. It was loaded with every kind of candy. And there were popcorn balls.

179

"Oh, thanks . . . a Coke," said Harry, distracted. He saw Hao trying to hide a suspicious expression in his eyes.

"What's going on, Hao?" Harry asked.

"We're just waiting for the scream."

"What scream?" Harry asked.

"The scream that comes from the big, fat mouth of Titus Kligore once he gets his fill of every terrible thing he ever did to any of us plus Scream One, Two, Three, and Four." Hao popped a Hershey's Kiss striped in Halloween orange and black into his mouth.

"Where is he?" Harry asked.

"In the Cube."

"In the Cube? I warned you guys," Harry said.

"Hey, did you hear him?" asked Hao.

"How can anyone hear anything with the music so loud?" Harry shouted.

"We had to turn it up so old man Kligore wouldn't stop us. We have him in the party-favor room telling tales to his adoring fans," Bailey said with a smirk. "Hey, did you hear it that time?"

"Hear what? The Cube only allows for one scream," Harry said.

Sarah walked over with the Cokes and handed one to Harry. "What's that screaming?"

"You hear it?" said Hao.

"I have sensitive ears," Sarah said. "Is it a new ride or something? There's an awful lot of screaming!"

Hao laughed. "That's because Larry the Locksmith overrode the security door. Fat-mouth Titus is not getting out from that slammer of horror anytime soon."

"Whaddaya mean?" asked Harry.

181

"He robbed you of your glory, Harry. We don't like that. He and his dad have this town trick-wired for their own pleasure."

"He was good tonight. All the Maniacs were!" Harry said.

"Yeah. But you, Sarah, and Rabbit blew it up! Hey! Where is Rabbit, anyway? Is he coming by for a Coke or is he still somewhere up in the atmosphere?"

Not even the music could mask the now

constant shouting. Harry looked across the makeshift dance floor and the sea of dancers. He could see that the Cube was not only rattling—it was rocking from side to side.

It was rumbling with such crazy energy that all the kids had moved away from it.

Then it happened. There was a low sounding explosion when the Cube erupted into flames. It took but an instant before the fire licked up the wall of Halloween costumes. Highly flammable, the costumes fired up in vivid orange and yellow. The flames hit the net on the ceiling, loaded with scary stuff. As the flames from the Cube tore at the nylon netting, skeletons, plastic gravestones, spiders, bats, and stuffed zombies fell onto the dancers.

Party guests screamed and ran in every direction. "Fire! Fire!" They screamed.

Larry the Locksmith jumped onto the side of the Cube. He pulled and banged at the door. It wouldn't budge. The door was too hot and burned his hands. "I can't open it!" he called. "Help!"

As kids ran out of the store to escape the fire and the falling skeletons, Sarah grabbed Harry.

"You have to do something!" she screamed.

Harry grabbed Sarah's hands. He looked into her frightened eyes. His heart pounded. "What can I do? I may be wearing a cape, but I am not Superman."

"No, you're better than Superman—you are real. Use your magic, Harry Moon. Save your enemy. Save Titus!"

"You're right," he said. "I have to save him." Harry looked toward the Cube, now nearly one hundred percent engulfed in flames.

She reached down and turned his face to hers. "I believe in you," she whispered to him.

"I can do this," he said. He ran toward the Cube.

"Be careful!" Sarah shouted.

Getting to Titus was not easy. The crowd was still running, the ceiling was on fire, and the showroom was filling with smoke. Taylor

Dingham, the school's best linebacker, clobbered Harry in the chin with his right elbow, unable to see as he ran for his own life. As Harry fell to the floor, Wand went flying. Reaching blindly through the smoke, he called for the wand.

"Wand to me," he commanded. "Wand!" And there it was—tight in his fingers! Wand's obedience to him gave him confidence. Harry clambered to his feet. His knees shook but the straighter he stood, the stronger he grew.

Harry opened his arms with the wand in his right hand. "A B R A C A D A B R A!"

Suddenly, Harry was standing on top of the flaming cube. He groped around for the door handle. He couldn't be sure if he found it or not. The handle was cold to the touch. He waved the wand in front of his eyes, and he could see past the smoke. He yanked on the handle, but it did not budge.

He waved the wand over his hand. He again reached for the handle, but it had disappeared. In its stead was a hole. He reached inside the opening and pulled at the surface of the door. In his hand, the thick metal became tin. He peeled it back from the Cube as if he was opening a can of sardines.

He could hear Titus cough. Harry gasped. *He's alive!* He stepped into the Cube, thinking of Titus's mean behavior to so many. Harry thought of Titus's own cruel acts to him— especially that terrible assault on the sidewalk on Nightingale Lane. Harry hesitated, even though Titus was crying—calling for help.

He must be worth saving, Harry thought. *Otherwise, my magic couldn't work. Right?*

"Right!" said the voice of Rabbit.

"There must be some good in him, right?" Harry said.

"There is good in everyone," Rabbit's voice answered, "but some people just don't know how to find it."

"I'm over here," said Titus's faint voice from behind a smashed LED screen.

"Coming! Be right there," Harry assured Titus as he crawled toward the groans.

Titus looked up at the screen in front of him. Rising above the screen like a morning sun on the horizon was Harry Moon.

Titus coughed. He rubbed his eyes and looked at the boy in the smoky air. "Harry? I don't believe it." He coughed again.

187

"It's me," Harry said.

"But I cut your hair off," said Titus, gasping for a breath of good air.

"It grows quickly," Harry replied. "Are you okay?"

"I think so."

Titus rubbed his soot-covered eyelids and looked back at Harry. He took the deepest breath he could and asked, "Who are you, Harry Moon?"

Harry reached his hand toward Titus. "Just a guy with a rabbit. Let's get outta here."

After what felt like an endless barrage of questions from the Sleepy Hollow Police and Fire Departments, Harry was free to go. With Titus safe, Harry stepped through the Chillie Willies administration office door and into the showroom. He swallowed hard and surveyed the damage. For the first time that night, Harry saw the danger he and Titus had faced. Tears threatened. But Harry sniffed them back.

The showroom was devastated. The once colorful shop was as gray and empty as the Sleepy Hollow Cemetery. Everyone was gone except for some firefighters checking for smoldering embers. Maintenance folk were sweeping up ashes and debris. As Harry crossed the floor, he could not help but think of the trouble his classmates faced.

When he reached the parking lot, he heard a shout. "Hey!"

"Hey?" he said softly into the darkness. He froze in midstride.

"Over here," said a girl's voice. "It's me."

Harry walked closer to the voice. "Sarah, I cannot believe you waited for me."

"No prob," said Sarah. "I drove . . . remember? My truck doesn't leave anybody behind."

Harry saw her moving toward him. As she came closer, the streetlights illuminated her scarves and her face. The bangles on her wrists shone. He saw a small wooden box sitting along the edge of the parking lot. He grabbed it quickly and placed it near his feet.

He stood on the box while she laughed.

"What are you doing, you big goof?" she asked as she reached him. Her face was flushed. He was very close. And for the first time, he could see her eye-to-eye.

"Straightening your diadem," he said. He reached out and arranged the golden tiara amidst her red hair. He fiddled with it for a moment, but she didn't seem to mind.

Then he looked at her, gathering the strands of hair away from her face.

"Someone once said to me that time changes everything."

"Uh-huh," she murmured.

"Sometimes that can happen all in a single moment."

She closed her eyes as Harry leaned in to kiss her on the lips. It was as if he walked into a dream.

As wonderful as he imagined it might be—it was that and more.

He may have stayed there a little too long, but she didn't seem to mind. Because when he pulled his lips from hers, she opened her eyes and smiled.

"Abracadabra, Harry Moon," she whispered. There seemed to be puffy blue clouds all around them. Harry smiled.

"A B R A C A D A B R A!" he replied.

191

192

Good Mischief

D ue to the fire at Chillies, the selectmen and Town Council convened on Sunday for a special sentencing of the teens who admitted they were involved in the Haunted Cube incident. These included

Clooney Mackay, Bailey Wheeler, Declan Dickinson, and Hao Jones. The sheriff, firefighters, teachers, and half the town were there to decide what to do with the kids. The dramatists at Sleepy Hollow Middle School talked jail time. The athletes discussed controlled hazing. The moderates won with detention. It was for six weeks . . . every afternoon after school and every Saturday.

After the meeting had broken up, Harry met Bailey, Declan, and Hao just before their parents hauled them home to begin their sentence. "That was rough," Harry said. "But you guys had to know what you were doing was not right."

Bailey looked at his high tops. "We were just trying to look out for you, Harry. But no more."

"Right," Hao said.

"I'm through with bad mischief," Bailey said. "I've never been so scared in my life. Titus could have died."

"And we could've ended up in jail," Hao said.

Harry looked at his friends. Glad they had admitted their guilt, he was also convinced he had to do something long-lasting. "Hey guys," he said, "let's really mean it now. Let's truly be the Good Mischief Team."

"Sounds great," Bailey said just before his father grabbed his arm and led him to the car.

195

Harry looked around the crowd. He saw Clooney Mackay standing with his father. Harry knew it was his dad's laptop that burned in the fire. He was also one of the only people in Sleepy Hollow who knew how Clooney's father punished him. Clooney had the welts from the buckle strap to prove it. But Clooney told anyone else who saw the welts that he got them in the mayhem of the Haunted Cube incident.

When Harry heard the lie that Clooney told everyone about his welts, he thought about how unfair life could be. Rabbit was right. These were troubled times. *Maybe there will always be trouble,* thought Harry. *So why not try and be a hero?*

As Harry walked to school Monday morning, he thought how fortunate he was to have a mom and dad who maybe didn't always seem to like him but always loved him. He was fortunate to have a dad who never hit him and whose worse fault was to make silly silk screens of Harry's sometimes stupid sayings and pass them out to his friends . . . like "No more training wheels for me" or "I wear sunscreen even though I am a Moon."

When Harry got to homeroom, everyone was already in their seats—highly unusual. Even Declan and Bailey, who always walked with Harry but had to get to school early, were in their assigned seats. Harry sat down, and Miss Pryor, also his homeroom teacher, closed the door. She walked to the front of the classroom and stood behind her desk, next to her bust of Shakespeare, "the Genius," as she called him.

"Students, as you know, I oversaw the Scary Talent Show this fall as I always do. On Saturday night, everyone did well, but our Harry Moon was exceptional—not only because of his talents but because of his strength of character in the way he handled the unfortunate technical ruling regarding his performance. I think we should give him a round of applause."

The students clapped for Harry. He nodded. Then Clooney Mackay stood and faced Harry. He was wearing his DO NO EVIL silk-screened T-shirt. He nodded to Harry. *That means a lot to me*, Harry thought. *Clooney has a tough life, but he is stepping up.* Behind Clooney, his girlfriend, PJ McDonald, stood as well. She, too, wore the DO NO EVIL T-shirt. She smiled at Harry as she applauded.

Bailey stood next. Harry turned and saw Declan standing too. *Geez*, Harry thought. *One day I am going to get my dad for all this stuff.* Each student wore a custom silk-screened T-shirt with DO NO EVIL, courtesy of the Moon garage.

One by one, each student stood until Harry Moon was surrounded by a sea of students. Harry got a little choked up. But the most surprising moment of all came when the tallest student in eighth grade stood at the

back of the class. Harry could not believe his eyes. Harry blinked. Standing like a tall ship in the Boston Harbor was Titus Kligore. Upon his sail, in black stenciled paint, were the words from Harry's dream—DO NO EVIL. Harry watched in disbelief as Titus winked. Not only did he wink, but he smiled too.

The whole class stood with their DO NO EVIL T-shirts. They looked at Harry. They applauded him. Everyone wore a DO NO EVIL T-shirt.

Yes! Harry thought. *We all are here to do no evil!* Harry could not help but think this was a new beginning for the Good Mischief Team.

After a few moments, Miss Pryor settled the class and got on with the business of school. She only had a few announcements before the bell rang and everyone scrambled to get to first period.

When Harry stopped at his locker to grab his algebra book, Titus headed over to him. "Harry, I just want to thank you for what you did."

"No sweat," Harry said. He felt a tad uncomfortable. Titus stayed glued to his side as he rummaged through his locker looking for his math book.

"Are you all right?" Harry asked.

"Yeah," Titus said. "The EMTs made me go to the hospital to get checked out. Your mom was my nurse. She said I was strong as an ox."

Harry laughed. "That's my mom."

"Also, I want to apologize for being so terrible to you for these past eight years," Titus said.

"Nine years. Don't forget kindergarten."

"Nine years then. I am sorry. I really am. Someone told me that when you almost die, you can have an epiphany."

"Did you?" Harry asked. "Have an epiphany?"

"Sure did. It might sound strange, but I thought about Abraham Lincoln and his sad story. And what he said about it."

Harry pushed his algebra book into his backpack. "What did he say, Titus?"

"Well, it was more like a question," Titus said. "Lincoln asked, 'what's the best way to get rid of an enemy'?"

"I don't know," Harry said. "Did Abraham Lincoln have an answer?"

"Lincoln said, 'The best way to get rid of an enemy is to make him your friend,'" Titus explained.

201

Harry closed his locker. He wasn't exactly sure how to respond. It was definitely not like Titus to be so nice. "I like that," Harry said. "Just don't tell my dad. Otherwise, we will all be wearing that on a T-shirt."

Titus laughed. Harry laughed too. They shared their laughter together. In that moment, everything changed for both Harry and Titus. Now it was the ghouls and ghosts and the Headless Horseman that were scarier than their classmates at Sleepy Hollow Middle School.

"That's what you did to me," Titus said. "I was your enemy, but you treated me like a friend. One day, I hope we can be friends, Moon."

Harry didn't answer right away. After all, Titus had committed many terrible acts against him, including the impromptu haircut. He thought it best to tread slowly; trust was something to be earned. But he also knew that Rabbit would have a lot to say about loving his enemies. "Okay, Titus," Harry said. "Let's work on it. Let's start today. In our little, spooky town of Sleepy Hollow, there's plenty of trouble, so let's try to work together."

Titus smiled, and he and Harry walked to algebra together. And this time, Titus didn't make a single remark about Harry's size or his name. And Harry was glad for that. But he was also not entirely convinced Titus was one hundred percent changed. Still, Harry felt good that day. It was a very good day. He had made a new friend . . . well, almost a new friend. He felt ready for life. He even felt ready for school. Yes, there would be lots more paper in his life. But there were no more scissors. At least no more shears upon his inky, black hair. Now, he had not only Rabbit but he also had Wand. And for Harry Moon, if it came down to a choice, he would not choose a rock, paper, or scissors.

He would choose the deep magic that was in him, magic that would continue to grow like Rabbit told him, magic that was in all of us if

only we had the soul to see it. That day, Harry no longer felt like a tourist who saw only with his eyes. He was a traveler who also saw with his spirit. That day, the world looked good. Even Titus was okay. *Rabbit was right. There was goodness in every one of us.*

That day, Harry had a glimpse of his destiny. To fight evil with good. To be on the lookout for chances to practice his good magic and show others the path to the deep magic. Harry Moon was a traveler now, and he wanted to take as many people along with him as he could, including the Good Mischief Team and maybe even, one day, Titus Kligore.

Harry might not have won the Scary Talent Contest. That was all right with him. What Harry Moon won that night was way more important. He was no longer scared. He had replaced fear with courage. Darkness may have found a home in Sleepy Hollow, but if young Harry Moon had anything to say about it, darkness would not be staying.

Rock-Paper-Scissors? Let the magic begin.

My Dear Readers,

Thank you for traveling with me into the world of Harry Moon. I love Harry Moon. I love everything about him. I love his name. I love his magic. And most of all, I love his courage.

I was never the most popular kid in school. I spent a lot of my time in a barn when I was in middle school taking care of my rabbits. I think I was always a little bit on the outside of things.

Maybe that's why I relate to Harry so much. He has what it takes to stand up for what is right and isn't afraid to do the hard thing, even as an outsider. That's pretty cool. Of course, he also gets to kiss the prettiest girl in the room, which is not too shabby.

In life, we need a real friend like Rabbit. There is a lot of value in knowing someone who is wise, who can help you through the tough times. That's the point, I think, of these amazing adventures—life is better when you've got a friend who can help point the way.

I am happy that you have decided to come along with me in these amazing adventures of Harry Moon. I would love for you to let me know if there are any fun ideas you have for Harry in his future stories. Go to harrymoon.com and let me know. Also, please join me on YouTube in the Rabbit Room.

See you again in the next adventure of Harry Moon!

Love,

Mark Andrew Poe

Harry Moon's
DNA

Helps his fellow schoolmates
Makes friends with those who had once been his enemies
Respects nature
Honors his body
Does not categorize people too quickly
Seeks wisdom from adults
Guides the young
Controls his passions
Is curious
Understands that life will have trouble and accepts it
And, of course, loves his mom!

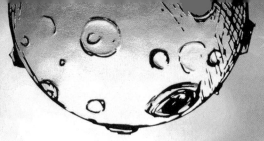

COMING SOON!
MORE MAGICAL ADVENTURES

POSTER INSIDE!

HARRY MOON

HALLOWEEN NIGHTMARES

MARK ANDREW POE

POSTER INSIDE!

HARRY MOON
HARRY'S CHRISTMAS CAROL

POSTER INSIDE!

HARRY MOON
TICKLISH

MARK ANDREW POE

POSTER INSIDE!

HARRY MOON
PROFESSOR EINSTONE

POSTER INSIDE!

HARRY MOON
FIRST LIGHT

MARK ANDREW POE

Honey Moon's
DNA

Builds friendships that matter
Goes where she is needed
Helps fellow classmates
Speaks her mind
Honors her body
Does not categorize others
Loves to have a blast
Seeks wisdom from adults
Desires to be brave
Sparkles away
And, of course, loves her mom